COME OUT & PLAY

PATRICK TUMBLETY

UNCOMFORTABLY DARK HORROR

"A unique and compelling tale. Tumblety's voice is one I suspect we'll be hearing for quite some time, and its arrival is a cause for celebration. Highly recommended!"—Brian Bowyer, Splatterpunk Award-nominated and Godless Award-winning author of OLD TOO SOON and METRO KINETIC

"Patrick Tumblety wrote a beautifully painful and action-packed tale with Come Out and Play. As a reader, I was both breathless from the insistent movement of the tale and I was grief stricken for the main character. Masterfully written and engrossing, this story is one not to be missed."—Somer Canon, author of You're Mine

"With COME OUT AND PLAY, Patrick Tumblety has created that most compelling of horror stories—an intriguing, gory spin on a beloved trope, peopled with fully realized characters who touch your heart, and a poignant look at how our trauma bleeds into every part of our lives. My heart didn't know whether to break or race—Tumblety is as gifted as they come."— Laurel Hightower, author of CROSSROADS and THE DAY OF THE DOOR

DEDICATION

Dedicated to my daughter,
Evelyn Rose Tumblety
You will never have to face the monsters alone.

Contents

PROLOGUE

RUINS

SCOTT HOLLAND STRAIGHTENS HIS necktie for the tenth time that morning as he walks across the street toward the church. A line of parishioners snakes up the marble staircase and through the open double-door entranceway made of oak. Holly leaves are chiseled around the frame and around the apex, where they encircle two cherub faces staring down toward the two-tiered steps. He stops at the first step and looks at the church's spires, silhouetted by the mid-morning sun. The gothic architecture resembles less "God's Sanctuary" and more like "Dracula's Castle." It might as well be, as terrified as he is to enter. He checks his tie again and then proceeds up the staircase.

A bald man in a white robe with gold trim greets each visitor before stepping inside. He halts the line when he sees Scott and offers a hand. Scott takes it and shakes, his hand nearly crushed under the man's strength.

"Your mother was a dear friend of the church, and to me. If you or your father need anything, please know that we are here for you. I'm Father Daniel, and here every Sunday for Mass."

The man's care seems genuine, although his words are suspicious. Scott has never known his mother to attend a church service, nor had she ever shown interest. He assumed she was being buried in a churchyard because she had been raised Catholic and her parents wanted to uphold the tradition. If this man knew his mother, he didn't seem bothered by her absence over the last seventeen years.

"Thank you," whispers Scott, because his voice has cracked every time he has tried to speak over the last few days.

The crowd parts to allow Scott to enter. He has been in churches before, for his cousins' baptisms, or his aunt's second wedding, and every time he steps foot into one, his senses need a moment to adjust. The interior - its history, culture, architecture that is anachronistic to the surrounding suburbia - is so foreign to him that walking into a church feels like moving into another realm with its own atmosphere.

Light filters through the stained-glass windows and splashes a kaleidoscope of brilliant colors across the stone pillars and marble flooring. He moves over to the baptismal font and pretends to dip his fingers into the water just in case anyone is looking. He stops making the sign of the cross when he realizes none of the mourners in the pews are facing backward. Some heads are bowed, while the others stare straight ahead at the casket in the church's crossing.

The oak doors slam behind him and darken the interior by half its light. With fewer means of escaping, he begins his treacherous journey up the nave, darting his eyes into every corner of the church except for his destination. The pillars are interconnected by arches along the ceiling, and a glass dome directly above the altar is showing a clear blue sky, allowing the morning sun to shine onto the casket.

None of the mourners acknowledge him as he passes. Not even his grandparents, whose sobbing has grown, bouncing across the stone and filling the space. Did they notice him and become triggered by his presence?

God, please right this wrong, they pray. *Take this evil boy away.*

The casket lies six feet from the nave, where he stops and takes a moment to prepare for his approach.

The altar sits on a rise above the casket, and beyond that hangs a crucifix on the back wall. It is big enough to touch from floor to ceiling, but he has not noticed it until now. The figure is sculpted in fine detail. The pale skin color is enhanced with varying hues of white, and covers an emaciated frame with realistic structure and shadowing. The beard is carved from a darker wood, with long black lines to add depth to the hair. Jesus's eyes point towards the sky, his expression sorrowful. Lines of red have been painted where the thorns in the crown touch his temple.

He feels countless eyes staring at him as he closes the space to the casket. He places his hands on top of the lacquered wood and bows his head. He has cried into dehydration over the last several days and has become numb, physically and mentally. He wonders how many of his family and friends are horrified by his lack of sorrow. He traces the wood's grain with his eyes until he feels enough time has passed for him to move on.

As he turns to leave, two heads in the second row rise in unison. His closest friends, Sarah Alaway and Chris Wells. Their eyes look directly into his. They do not offer sympathy or empathy. They offer anger.

Of course, they are angry. She was a mother to them, too.

Sarah's eyes lift toward the ceiling and then widen. Her face drains of color and her mouth opens to scream, but no sound releases.

Scott turns. The only objects in front of him are the casket, the pulpit, the altar, and the crucifix. He turns back around to ask Sarah what scared her, but the space she occupied is empty. Chris is still there, but he's no longer sitting straight. Half of his body is slumping over the first pew.

"Hey!" Scott yells to get someone's attention, but no one rises from their reverie.

The feeling of eyes on him returns, even though all the heads he sees are still bowed. A screeching sound comes from behind him. He turns to find the casket has opened.

His mother's body is not there.

He looks around to see how someone has been able to abscond with a body, but no one else is there—

The crucifix steals his attention.

Something about it has changed. The scratched skin around the thorns seems darker. The lines of blood that stem from them seem longer. The harder Scott concentrates on the wounds, the clearer the details become. The thorns are more lifelike than he realized, pitted and irregular. The skin tone is colored with more imperfections, like pockmarks and bruises. The ribcage and clavicle are sucked in, cavernous, draped with impossibly thin skin. The beard is fully detailed with so many variations of color that it resembles real hair. Jesus' face is no longer sorrowful, but contorted in agony. His eyes are wider, his mouth open. A scream without sound.

The change is so alarming that he thinks something might be wrong with his mind, having viewed the statue so differently at first glance. Has grief twisted his perception? His heart races and his hands shake. He pulls at the knot around his neck and loosens it, but continues to feel like he cannot intake enough air. He looks up toward the crucifix and hopes that it looks the same as when he first noticed it. Proof of his sanity.

The statue's face is staring down at him.

He backs away, but his feet trip over themselves and send him to the floor. As he stands, he looks back toward the statue. The statue's upper body is leaning away from the cross and hovering directly above him.

Scott turns and runs down the aisle.

"Somebody help!" He screams at the plethora of mourners filling the pews, but not one of them reacts. He looks around for someone he recognizes - his father, aunts, uncles, cousins, his neighbor Mr. Shirley - anyone familiar. He turns his head toward where his grandparents had been sitting, but they continue to pray, ignoring his pleas.

He continues to run but risks another look back. He sees that the cross remains on the wall, but the body stands in front of the casket.

Terror threatens to take the strength from his legs, but he pushes through it until he reaches the oak doors. His body slams into one side, but it does not open. He slams against the other door, but it also does not budge. Pain shoots through his shoulder, but he does not let it slow him down. He plants his feet and pivots his body so that he can lean into the door with full strength. Before he thrusts forward, he chances a glance down the aisle to see how much time he has left.

The statue's face is inches from his own.

Instead of a tortured expression, its smile stretches unnaturally from ear to ear. Its mouth is open, unleashing the stench of bile and heat so hot that it singes Scott's cheek. Large rows of canine-like teeth grow in length around the black void that is the inside of its mouth. A deep, echoing voice rises from within.

"Amen."

Chapter One

Step on that crack, you'll break your mother's back!

Scott's foot hesitates over the split in the concrete and then steps on the other side of it, just in case. In case of what, he has no idea. Even so, the spiderweb of fissures that lie before him and stretch across the basement floor might as well be one hundred Grand Canyons to hurdle.

A single bulb hangs above the washer and dryer, casting yellow light barely bright enough to reach into the opposite corners of the room. Groundwater seeps through the fissures in the concrete walls. Splinters of wood litter the ground from the crumbling stairway along with the dust that has loosened from wood support beams along the ceiling. Cobwebs stretch across metal shelves and the assorted groceries they hold. Even as a child, Scott understood why basements are a common trope in horror movies. A basement is colder than the rest of the house, has a separate smell and temperature, and is home to the creepiest of crawlies. Worst of all, a basement is buried inside the earth, a grave for old things.

Exactly where you should be.

Two cribs sit at the back of the room. Their posts strain against an overabundance of mementos, keepsakes, and souvenirs from different eras of his family's history.

A heavy set of encyclopedias.

Plastic candy-cane decorations for the lawn.

Donatello, the Ninja Turtle and Peter the Ghostbuster — heroes whose colors are muted under a thick layer of dust.

A child's tattered mummy costume, the wrapping sewn together by his grandmother's hands when trick-or-treating was new and mythical.

He grabs one of the posts and pulls, but it does not budge. He leans back and kicks it with his bare heel. It snaps more easily than he expects and sends his foot into the avalanching pile. He frees his leg before a heavy-framed portrait of his mother slides down and nearly collides with his ankle. Until three months ago, the portrait had been hanging in the stairway in the living room that leads up to his bedroom. His father must have thrown it onto the pile so he wouldn't have to look at it, or maybe to keep Scott from looking at it every time he went up to his room. Mom's portrait should not have been cast down with these miscellaneous items. He can almost tell that her face in the photograph is full of disapproval. He pulls it from the mound and leans it against the wall with care and respect.

"Last in, first out," his mother would iterate while he was cleaning his toys and wanting his favorites to still be accessible.

The rest of the items have piled up over the course of several years. Every time his mother would tell him to clean his room, Scott would quip under his breath, "Why not just throw it in the basement?"

Heavy rain flooded the room a week ago and the water damage is still apparent. His father wants him to store whatever is salvageable in plastic bins and throw away the rest.

A clay imprint of Scott's first steps, now crumbling under the weight of the proceeding years.

A composition notebook scrawled with his first book report - a Goosebumps book called Welcome To Dead House - is soggy and unreadable.

A silver bracelet with a triceratops charm his father had bought him on one of their family vacations at the shore. Tarnished, with half its links cracked.

Why have you abandoned us in this cold, dark place? They croon.

"I'm sorry," replies Scott, with equal parts remorse for them and ridicule for himself for thinking that inanimate objects have feelings.

The floor above creaks. Dust falls from the ceiling.

"I'll come back to clean you up, I promise," he tells the hoard of memories.

They don't believe you.

Shadow is waiting for him as he opens the door into the main hallway. The cat meows like he has not eaten in days.

"All right, you monster, let's eat." He shuts the basement door and heads down the hallway with his black cat in tow. He enters the kitchen and notices that his father has not yet started brewing the coffee. Making a pot before his father leaves for work is the least Scott can do in light of their new living situation, so he grabs the glass jar of coffee beans from the counter and tips it into the grinder.

The image from his mother's portrait refuses to leave his mind's eye, but having no image of her in the house makes his stomach churn. Even though it will pain the men until they are ready to deal with the loss—

Don't!

Beans topple over the grinder, roll across the counter, and cascade onto the floor. They bounce across the tile while creating the sound of a rainstorm.

Scott places his hand on his temple and closes his eyes, waiting for the rain to stop.

How many did you just waste?

He kneels and scoops the beans into a pile to try to grab as many as he can in one fistful.

Don't you dare! Put those down and then pick them up one at a time.

One by one, he picks the beans from the floor and returns them to the jar, their home. Some have rolled underneath the refrigerator, from where they might never return.

Let that be a reminder every time you open the fridge.

The door to the master bedroom pops open from the other end of the hallway.

"You should have stayed asleep," his father yells. "I have no presents for you."

"All I ask for is your love, Dad," Scott quips, trying to finish his penance before his father enters the room. His father laughs as he crosses the hall and enters the bathroom.

With the beans returned home, Scott starts brewing. He pours a bowl of Fruity Pebbles for himself and sits at the table. The newspaper lying there is from the day before, which means his father will be asking for today's edition. Pushing away the thought of being forced to go outside to retrieve it, he pinches through the pages, trying to avoid depressing headlines until he reaches the comics. The Family Circus is moving on with their boring lives. The Phantom is still protecting the jungle. Charlie Brown is still trying to figure it all out while his dog leads a more adventurous life.

The paper crinkles as Shadow paws it from the other side. The tip of his nail pokes through Garfield's head and slices it down the middle as if the two cats have a score to settle. Scott releases his hold on the paper, letting it crumble under the feline's weight as he sits on top. The cat stares his owner down with a contempt that only cats can display.

Scott sighs. "I'm sorry."

He grabs a can of food from the pantry and taps its contents into a tiny bowl that is etched with "The Cat From Hell" around its edge. Scott's father had given it to him as a joke for his twelfth birthday. His father hated cats, even though he was the one to bring Shadow home as a kitten for Scott's fifth birthday.

Shadow laps up his wet food and Scott returns to slurping his milk, angry at himself for making his cat wait to eat.

You're disappointing everyone and you've only been awake for an hour.

"Couldn't sleep last night?" his father yells from the bathroom.

"I slept fine," he lies. His father can hear him tossing and moaning through the vent that connected the bedrooms. He discovered how thin the walls were at fifteen when he made out with Tammy Myers heavily enough to raise parental concern. It was the first time he had done that much kissing with a girl. He was in heaven until his father burst into the room. Three years later, he still has not had a girl in his room, except for Sarah, of course.

Who never wants to see you again.

"I picked a bunch of the tomatoes," his father gargles from the bathroom with a mouth full of toothpaste. "Go give those to Mr. Shirley, and I might have a present for you when you get back."

"Shit," says Scott, closing his eyes and burying his face in his hands. "It's fine. It'll be fine."

He walks into the living room and gently grabs the doorknob.

"Three minutes," he assures himself. "It'll only take you three minutes. Probably less."

Anything can happen in three minutes.

He rests his forehead on the oval window in the center of the wooden door and looks out onto Village Court. A basket of his mother's tomatoes sits on the porch that his father had picked from the plant bed in the backyard. She started growing them before she died, and they have finally come to fruition. Scott had heard rummaging around the outside of the house last night but figured it was raccoons trying to claw inside, maybe realizing the heat is about to drop and finding a place to get warm.

Seasons in New Jersey change without warning, and with August nearly over, the cold can come any minute. The morning dew is a harbinger of an early fall.

Beyond the door he hears lawnmowers singing their death knells, consuming what will surely be their last warm meal before hibernating in garages for the winter. He wants nothing more than to smell the freshly cut grass that awakens the freedom and peace of summer.

It's still hot outside, he thinks. It's a nice day. Going outside might help you relax.

Or you'll cause a whole new slew of problems.

A high-pitched voice calls from somewhere in the neighborhood. Through the window he sees Nancy Miller and her ten-year-old son David from the house next door, carrying bags of trash to the curb. Mrs. Miller has been having "the little man" do chores since he turned double-digits.

Across from the Miller's on the other side of the street stand Karen Campbell and her eight-year-old, Elisa, hauling grocery bags from their car. "Hi!" yells David, waving at Elisa as she struggles to carry a paper bag across the driveway. Elisa drops it and glass clangs from within. Her mother rushes to check whatever was in the bag did not break as her little girl waves her hands excitedly at the boy across the street.

There was a time when Scott would have run outside and helped with the trash and the groceries, just as he had cut Mr. Shirley's lawn and taken out the elderly man's trash every week. He had even taken Bastion, the old man's Boxer, for weekly walks. The old man's lawn is nearly overgrown at the corner of the cul-de-sac these days. Dad has had to take over those basic chores when he gets the time.

For the better. You'd find a way to screw it up.

Rusty door hinges screech from the house directly across the street, jumpstarting his heart. For eighteen years, that sound would have him rush to put on his shoes and run outside before his best friend left her porch.

Sarah emerges from her house and walks barefoot across the lawn. She picks up the newspaper, and as she shakes the plastic wrapping from the morning dew, she glances toward his door.

Scott moves from the window.

Her afterimage is a ghost in his eyes. Was that longing on her face? Excitement?

Does it matter? She's better off without you.

Scott shakes away that thought. At least wave to her, he thinks, or crack open the door and say, "good morning." Do something to acknowledge your best friend. You owe her that.

You owe her a life without you.

Another screech. Scott looks back in time to see Sarah's door shutting.

A coffee bean crumbles under his foot as he steps back into the kitchen. The tile is nearly clean of them, save for two lying beneath the sink cabinets. His father sees Scott looking at them, so he kneels to pick them up.

"Thank you," Scott says.

His father ignores him and throws the two beans into the trash.

*Never to return hom*e.

Scott's cheeks flush and his hands shake as he considers taking the beans out, washing them, and returning them to the jar to calm the headache growing in his head.

"Open this before I leave," his father says, picking a wrapped package off the kitchen counter and throwing it onto the table. He then walks past Scott and down the hall toward the master bedroom.

The present is a good distraction until he can rescue the beans from the trash.

The box is wrapped with snowman-patterned paper. His father probably could not have found where Mom had stored the birthday rolls. Tearing at it reminds him of previous Christmas mornings, opening gifts while his parents cuddled on the couch, cradling mugs of hot coffee in their hands.

Underneath the wrapping is a Macy's t-shirt box, and Scott hopes that his father did not try to pick out clothes. Under the lid is clothing, but not what he expects. It's a white canvas jacket with brown cuffs and a thick, fuzzy brown collar. He had pointed it out to his parents when they were at the mall earlier that year.

"I'm impressed you remembered," calls Scott down the hallway. With everything his father had been through, Scott was surprised that his father even cared about his birthday, let alone exactly what he wanted. Scott slips his arms into the sleeves. The jacket is a perfect fit. The fuzzy collar is comfy and the white looks like...

You'll ruin it in a day.

"What's wrong?" his father asks as he returns to the kitchen. "Not the right fit?"

"There's a tag inside," he lies, pulling on the side of the jacket. "This is awesome, Dad. Thank you."

"You're welcome," he says as he pours coffee into a thermos. "I'll be gone until tomorrow night."

"Where are you going?"

"Nan and Pop's. They are helping me understand all the legal documents I have to sign for your mother's will." He waves in the air like the process is not a big deal and then changes the subject. "Keep working in the basement."

Scott's stomach clenches, but how could he say, "No?" Who else was there to do it?

"I'll drop off the tomatoes to Mr. Shirley on the way out," he sighs.

"It's okay, Dad. I can—"

"It's fine," says his father, holding up his hand, a gesture that Scott was introduced to before he can remember. It means that his father will not continue to talk about it.

"Your mother bought you a card at the beginning of the year. I made her wait until your birthday, which was stupid in hindsight. It's on our dresser. She would want you to have it." He grabs the back of Scott's neck and pulls his head against his chest and says, "Happy eighteenth." He kisses his son's forehead and then heads for the hallway, stopping at the entrance. His shoulders tense.

Yes, Scott thinks. Say something. Yell at me. Tell me how you really feel. Tell me it's all my fault. Tell me anything. Something.

His father continues to move toward the door and walk out of the house.

He can't even look you in the eye.

Scott watches from the bay windows in the living room as his father carries the basket to Mr. Shirley's porch.

What if this is the last time you'll ever see him?

Scott places his hands on his face and breathes in slowly, trying to clear his mind of all irrational thoughts. He hears his father's car start, drive off the street, and then fade.

Never to return again, perhaps?

Now that he is alone, the house needs to be fortified.

The front door. The sliding glass doors in the kitchen. The sliding glass doors in the guest room that lead to the backyard. Every window on both floors. They all need to be locked, opened, locked again, and then tested to make sure they will not budge. The door that leads to the basement does not have a lock, so he sticks a bottle on top of the knob in case someone breaks through the wall from the drainage sewer.

Once his home is physically locked, he sets up emotional security.

The rooms smell too much like his mother, so he sprays men's cologne around the house.

A towel needs to be draped over the mirror above the sink in the bathroom. Way too many superstitions about mirrors make him uneasy to even touch one of their surfaces. He doesn't believe in superstitions, not really, but he also knows that he cannot disprove that they are not true, so why chance it? At least that is his reasoning, although he does not like to think about the other reason he avoids reflective surfaces.

Others have described him as a "normal" looking person, although he suspects that they really mean to say "average". Not skinny, but not heavy. Short brown hair, blue eyes, no distinctive features. On the shorter side for his age's average, but not enough to notice unless someone was really looking.

And who would want to?

When he looks at his reflection, he doesn't see a "normal" person or any of those features that others describe. He sees a nose that is too pointy, hair that doesn't want to comb straight. Short enough to be ridiculed by his peers at school. In the mirror he sees something twisted, something that is not welcomed in the world and should never have been borne.

Every photograph on the first floor, from grandparents to friends, and even his baby pictures, needs to be turned away. The last picture he deals with is of Nan and Pop sitting on a small table next to the television. They are embracing and staring at him from within the frame.

You took our daughter away from us, their faces tell him.

Scott turns the picture around.

We still know you're there.

He places his finger on the top edge of the frame.

"I'm sorry," he says and takes his finger away.

Not good enough.

He returns his finger to the frame.

"I'm sorry," he repeats and removes his finger.

Do you want us to die, too?

He touches the frame again.

"I'm sorry," he repeats and removes his finger.

That's all you can do?

He touches the frame again.

"I'm sorry," he repeats, emphatically sending his sincere emotions into the picture. This time, when he lifts his finger, the tiniest amount of relief washes over him.

Satisfied and exhausted, he collapses on the couch and hopes the thought will pass entirely.

He presses the worn-down power button on the television's remote seven times, and then once more to make an even number. The screen brightens and shows a monstrous shark raging out of the sea to chomp on Roy Scheider.

It's a sign.

Watching horror movies with his father is one of his favorite memories—

He'll never want to do that again.

—and Jaws is their favorite.

What does this mean? Do you think he won't make it to wherever he's going?

Scott lifts the remote to turn off the TV.

What if turning it off is the wrong thing to do? Like you're turning off his life?

His head hurts, so he compromises by turning the TV back on but muting the sound.

He closes his eyes and tries to push away all thoughts and take a nap.

Instead, his mind drifts to Sarah.

To the end of May.

To that night.

⸺◈⸺

SARAH'S FACE WAS FLUSHED from the heat of alcohol. They had been drinking the scotch Scott snatched from his father's collection and cuddling on her bed, listening to music and talking about what they were going to do that summer.

"How late is it?" He asked.

"I don't know. Time is irrelevant when I'm with you."

He turned his head and stared at her profile. Her beautiful face.

"I love you," he said.

"I love you, too," she replied. Her expression changed. Her jaw steeled. Her eyes were serious and searching his face like she was getting ready to react to something and needed to be ready.

"You okay?" He asked.

She turned her face toward his, leaned forward, and pushed her lips against his lips.

He was so shocked he didn't return it. They had said so many "I love you's" since they were kids that he never thought the words would ever be followed by a kiss.

Sarah shuffled a few inches away from him toward the edge of her bed. She panted with nervous energy as her eyes searched his face to gauge his reaction.

Scott stayed still; his mouth slightly open, unsure of what to say to her for the first time... ever. He looked around the room for something to concentrate on other than her terrified eyes, but the amount of alcohol he drank made the room spin.

The alcohol! His mind declared.

Neither had been that drunk before, and he realized his father's scotch was probably not the best formula with which to start experimenting.

"Are you with me, Scott?" Sarah asked, her voice barely a whisper.

"Always," he answered.

Without losing her tension, she said, "I meant about my decision to kiss you, idiot."

He wanted to pretend to be surprised, as though the kiss came unexpectedly, but a weight of tension had been hanging between them for a few weeks. A few weeks for him, at least.

"I thought it was just me who felt different," he said.

"When did you start to notice?"

Scott recalled the last couple of weeks and tried to pin down the exact moment when the love he felt for Sarah in his heart gave way to butterflies in his stomach.

"Last weekend. When we were lying on the floor in your living room while we were watching When Harry Met Sally on TV. You laughed and then squeezed my thigh. At first, I thought you were just being playful, but your fingers lingered before you pulled away. I didn't know if the way you touched me was different for you too, or if I was just... being a guy. I never felt that way about you when you touched me before and didn't know where it came from."

"No, you're right. I was acting differently." She lifted herself onto her elbow. "That guy Danny, from Algebra Two, asked me out a few weeks ago. I was totally ready to hook up with him, of course, but every time I thought about it, I considered how you would feel."

"You thought I'd be jealous?"

"Would you be?" she asked, her eyes searching for an answer.

"Not jealous, but... I'd hate having to spend less time with you. You've dated other people before and never mentioned any of this. What changed your mind?"

"At first I thought it was hormones. We spend all our time together. Sleep in the same bed most nights. I'm sure you felt the urge, too. We're teenagers. The feeling usually goes away the next day, but lately... it hasn't. It's been lingering. Then when Danny asked me out, I thought about being with him on a date, being romantic and smiling and laughing with him, and it felt wrong. It felt like I was cheating on you."

He reached out and grabbed one of her shaking hands. "I've never seen you like this before."

"I'm scared that telling you this changes everything. I never felt this way, and our relationship is so unique that any change we make might ruin something special."

Scott thought about it. "It does, unfortunately."

She swallowed hard and closed her eyes. "Fuck. What did I do?"

"Nothing," he assured her. "If anything, you might have started something great."

She opened her eyes and revealed sheens of water forming across them. "Are you saying that you feel the same way?"

"I've loved you since the first time you handed me a lump of mud and told me it was ice cream."

"But you're not in love with me?"

"Are you in love with me? For certain?"

She breathed deeply and let it out, along with a few tears. "I don't know. I usually know exactly how I feel about everything, but I don't know this. That's what makes me believe it's true."

Her eyes are red, her face is flustered, and although Scott does not want to admit it, he thinks he knows why she is so confused. Mostly, he just does not believe he deserves to be loved by her, and wants to give her a chance to take it back before his heart becomes hopeful. "How about we discuss it tomorrow when we're sober?"

"Probably for the best," she relented. "What do we do about tonight?"

"Tonight, we do what we always do. We cuddle until we fall asleep."

Scott held her tightly and listened to the silence in the dark room. Inside his head, he was screaming. The joy he felt from her confession, the reciprocation of a deeper love he had always felt for her but never described in words, was finally coming true.

No good can come from this.

The prospect of greater happiness also promised devastation for the happiness he already had. But for her? Would the risk of losing her be greater than the risk of never knowing what they could become? He thought about the question for several hours and still did not have an answer when sleep took him down.

"I don't feel different," he said through a headache and stomach cramps. "Other than the hangover."

"Me either," she said, holding herself back from throwing up.

They laughed at their misery and then decided to try to go on a date. They would do the same things they always did, such as grab food, go to the movies and the mall, but with an understanding that it would be as an official date with a capital D, to see how it felt.

That weekend, Scott told his mother he was going to take Sarah to the movies.

"You need at least six more months under your belt before you drive without me," she said while watching TV on the couch, flippantly waving a hand in the air as though what her son had said was preposterous.

Scott's hands were shaking, and his knees grew weak, but he steadied his voice and plainly stated, "I wasn't asking."

His mother muted the television and looked at him. "Don't talk to me like that. If you walk out of that door, you will be grounded. You're not eighteen yet, and even when you are, I'm still driving with you until I know you're ready."

There was no logical reason for his mother to be worried. He aced the driver's test, never challenged the speed limits, and always took time to change lanes. He made all the right moves while his mother was his backseat driver, so why didn't she trust him to do it on his own?

Scott gathered all the willpower he could muster to keep from looking away from her. "I'll be home by ten."

She followed him out of the door and hurled screams of protest from the porch. His father joined her. She was angry, so his father became angry, even though he did not know the subject of the argument. "Do what your mother tells you or you will get that car taken away."

Sarah was halfway across the lawn when the eruption began. She froze until Scott rolled his eyes and signaled politely for her to get into the car.

⸻ ◆ ⸻

ON THEIR WAY TO the movies, Sarah placed her hand on his shoulder until his tears dried.

"I'm sorry," he said, trying to hold back the quiver in his voice.

"Don't be," she replied. "Let it out."

He parked in front of the theater. She leaned over the gear shaft and cupped his face in her hands to kiss him gently on the lips.

"I will always be here for you." She wiped the remaining tears from his cheeks.

"What if this doesn't work?"

Her face hardened. "Always," she said. "No compromises."

"No compromises," he promised.

They leaned in for a kiss at the same time. They kissed, deeply. A new way of showing their love. A way to mark their new way of being together. The first time they ever said "Hello" to each other, they had said it in unison. It made sense to them that their passion should also be in harmony.

They skipped the movie in favor of dinner at their favorite diner. How could they sit in silence after the kiss they just shared? As usual, they talked about anything and everything, from deciding on the best pop song of the last one hundred years to the accuracy of Freud's dream interpretations. The only break in conversation was between bites of fries.

"Nothing is different," Scott said, "but everything feels different."

Sarah nodded. "I was thinking the same thing. It's... different," she laughed.

"I can tell. You've never been at a loss for words. I feel honored to be the one to make you so flustered," he laughed.

"Shut up," she said as she threw a French fry at his forehead.

"So, what do we do now that everything feels different?"

"Nothing," she replied.

His heart sank. "You don't think we should do... this?"

"No. I mean, let's just go with it. If it works, it does. If not, we can get through it. If two people can, we can."

"No compromises," he said.

She smiled. "None whatsoever."

Curfew had come and gone, but they didn't care. If there were two more responsible teenagers in the world, their parents could have those children instead.

This was a good decision, he thought, and with that thought, he decided that he would stop second-guessing his every action. Stay out of his head. Stay out of his way and just believe that good things can and will happen. With her by his side, he could control the outcome.

SOMETIME AFTER MIDNIGHT, THEY drove home while belting alt-rock in the car. A night that had started with such a confrontation turned out to be the most rewarding night of his life. He would go home and show his parents he was no worse for wear.

Scott rounded the corner of their cul-de-sac, disappointed that the night was about to end. "Are we still allowed sleepovers?" he asked with a laugh.

"What's going on?" Sarah asked, leaning forward to look out of the window.

"What do you mean?" Scott replied, still in a haze of romance.

Red and blue lights illuminated her face and grabbed his attention back to the road.

Two police officers were knocking on Scott's front door.

In a matter of minutes, they would tell him that his mother had died in a car accident.

She had been out looking for him, worried about his safety.

You killed your mother.

CHAPTER TWO

A STING OF PAIN in Scott's chest wakes him from sleep. He sits up and sees a line of red staining his white undershirt. Shadow stands on the glass coffee table with his back arched and head tilted, fur standing straight up and tail swaying back and forth.

"I'm sorry," he tells the cat, voice shaking through the remnants of the nightmare that continue to prick his skin. This was not the first time that the cat has pulled him from a nightmare, mewing directly in his ear or crawling across his chest. He lifts the back of his hand to allow the cat to sniff it. Shadow head-butts his knuckles and then lowers his arched back as he crawls onto Scott's lap.

"Thanks for looking out for me."

You don't deserve his protection.

Scott rakes shaky fingers up and down Shadow's fur and thinks about the nightmare. No matter how many times it returned, he still could not get used to the idea that it had happened.

Despite the memory, or maybe because of it, he takes another treacherous journey into the basement full of canyons to retrieve his mother's portrait. After ten minutes of careful stepping, he returns the frame to its nail in the stairway wall leading to his bedroom. He forces his eyes not to look away from her face even as his eyes burn from the layers of dust he brushes from the glass. The last emotion either of them saw on each other's faces was anger, so he might as well look at her now. Besides, she did not leave him; she had been taken. His pain should not matter more than her memory.

In the image, she sits on a rusted iron bench in the middle of a weed-choked garden. She is bent over, elbows on her knees, and holding her favorite piece of jewelry, a peridot stone in a silver pendant on a silver chain. She had not been buried with it and he does not know where that ended up. He assumes his father hid it for safekeeping. As she holds the charm, her face is melancholy, staring at something beyond the frame.

Scott remembers asking her why she looked so distant.

"I felt very lonely at that moment," she explained. "Your dad and I were cleaning your grandfather's house the week after he died, taking pictures of his final possessions to give away or sell. Your grandmother had died the week before, so he died alone. Dying alone, without at least one loved one, scares me more than anything."

"Will I be there when you die?" he asked.

"I hope so, Scott, so I can see your cute face one last time."

Scott was about ten years old when his mother told him that. It was the first moment he remembered becoming aware of and afraid of death.

Fresh tears well in his eyes, as they do every time he remembers he had brought his mother's greatest fear to life.

And now you have this as punishment.

It's not my fault, he thinks, while staring at his face through the glass's reflection. All he wanted was to take his best friend to the movies. He was a safe driver. He drove extra safely because Sarah was in the car.

It's not my fault.

Stop lying to yourself.

He pulls the picture from the wall, raises it above his head, and brings it down onto his knee. The glass cracks and the wood splinters. He raises it again and slams it back down until his kneecap numbs and blood seeps through his flannel pajamas.

Oh, good! You already killed her, now kill her memory.

The wood splinters on both sides and one-half of the frame falls to the floor. He pulls the picture from between the shattered glass, taking it in both hands and then taking a deep breath.

"You'll regret that," a voice warns him.

It takes a few seconds to realize that the voice isn't coming from his mind. He screams and turns around, dropping the picture onto the splintered wood and glass.

"Good afternoon?" Sarah asks, her voice indicating equal parts sarcasm and worry.

His heart beats quickly, not solely because she startled him. Every sense awakens in her presence. The grey canvas bag he had bought her for Christmas two years before still hangs from her shoulder, the strap across her chest. Her black hair has been trimmed from waist level to just below her shoulder. Her body has become toned and tanned from playing soccer throughout the summer. Her wrist is adorned with a braided leather thread. A friendship bracelet, most likely. How many friends did she make without him?

Probably several now that you're not there to scare them off.

"Honestly," he says, looking toward the floor and wiping the tears from his eyes, "I've had worse days. I'm sorry."

"Don't apologize to me," she nods toward the portrait.

"You don't believe in an afterlife."

"I don't believe in heaven or hell, but we all end up somewhere."

"What if there's nothing after this?"

"Then you have nothing to worry about."

Scott rolls his eyes. "Why are you here?" he asks.

"Rude," she says.

He lifts his hands into the air. "I think it's a solid question."

"It's your birthday," she answers like he has asked the dumbest question.

"Yeah," he pauses. "I didn't think you'd remember."

"I haven't forgotten for over ten years."

"I didn't think you'd care," he snaps and instantly regrets it. The humor drops from her face.

"I've been giving you space," she says, "until you invited me over."

"You never needed an invitation before."

"We've never been through anything like this before."

He wants her to clarify what she means by "this," but is afraid of the answer. There have been two big changes since the last time they were together. One was their love, and the other was his mother's life, both dying on the same night.

"What would you like to do?" she asks, pulling him out of his thoughts.

"I planned on cleaning."

"That's it?"

"Dad has had me sifting through Mom's hoardings in the basement all week. Next week it'll be the attic."

"Eww," she said. "How much have you gotten rid of?"

He averts his eyes.

"Want some help?"

Ever so slightly, he nods his head. "I wish I could do it on my own," he confesses.

She grabs his shoulder and squeezes. "You don't have to. We all have something to deal with. Yours is just a little more complicated at the moment. But is cleaning a grungy basement what you would like to do on your birthday?"

"Honestly, it would be the most productive thing I've done in a while."

"Lead the way. I'm all yours," she says with a raised eyebrow and a playful lilt in her voice. The eyebrow lowers, and this time she averts her eyes.

"Last one down is a rotten egg," Scott offers to ease the tension.

With her company, even the descent back down the stairs is easier. He watches her step through the cracks without care. She stops suddenly in the middle of the room and looks over the mess. "How long have you been at this?" she questions.

"I know. I'm just afraid to throw anything out."

"Why are you afraid?"

"Just a figure of speech."

"Most people would say they are sad to see things go or hope they can be salvaged. What makes you afraid?"

"I guess…" he searches for an answer, "if I throw these away, it's like losing more of Mom."

Sarah nods and turns toward the overflowing pile. She kneels and picks up a child's board book that's water-damaged enough to drown half of the puppy illustration on the cover. "I'm sure your dad just wants to clean up what isn't salvageable." She pinches the only dry corner and lifts it into the air. "How do you feel about throwing this away?"

"Like I'd be burying a body that was not really dead."

"It's an inanimate object, Scott. It's only alive in your head."

"My mother used to read that to me. If it's gone—"

"The memory is still alive in you."

She's right, he knows. However, the book is still there. It's rotting and unusable, but it's still there, so why would he choose to throw it away if some of it remains?

"Okay," she nods, noticing his furrowed brow, "here's what we're going to do. Put everything that is damaged into a box so it's at least out of the way, and then we can decide what to do with it later."

The idea of placing these memories into the equivalent of a casket gives him a wave of anxiety, but he grabs an empty plastic storage bin from one of the utility shelves.

They work in silence. Scott hopes it's because they are busy and not because they're avoiding the obvious conversation they will need to have. These months without her have been painful, not just because of the way they parted, but because she is the one who always heals his wounds. They used to be a whole person while they were together. Trying to become closer - or rather a different kind of close - had immediately torn them apart.

You should have left well enough alone.

Is that what happened? Had he pushed his luck too far?

A bang from above causes the ceiling to shake. They turn down their faces to avoid the falling dust.

"That was the side door," Scott says.

"You think someone broke in to rob the place?" she asks. "Here?"

"What else could it be?" The only real trouble in the neighborhood was bicycles being stolen and houses egged. Still, he takes the stairs slowly, trying not to squeak the wood to alert the intruder. No one who has a key - Mr. Shirley, Sarah's parents, or his grandparents - has visited without his father at home since the accident.

No one wants to be around a murderer.

At the top of the stairs, he turns the doorknob and slowly pushes the door. Through the narrow opening, he sees the pink hue of dusk bleeding into the house from the sliding glass door in the kitchen. A piece of paper blows off the table and floats to the floor at the entranceway between the tile and carpet.

An owl's coo heralds the night. The door is open even though he knows he locked it. Several times.

The fear of an intruder becomes secondary as he realizes that Shadow could escape. He runs into the kitchen and slides the door home. He locks it again but knows that he can't repeat the process because whatever he is locking it against is already inside.

A figure in the door is reflected behind him, larger than Sarah and wearing something brighter. Scott is too slow to turn before arms wrap around him and push his face against the cold glass.

Lips brush against the back of his ear, releasing hot breath that carries the scent of alcohol.

"Boo," the intruder whispers.

As Scott recognizes the voice, the tip of a moist finger enters his ear. "Ugh. Really?"

Scott is released from the grasp. Chris is grinning ear to ear, an overgrown child.

"Oh, that was nothing," the larger man says while smacking a thick hand on Scott's shoulder. "I still owe you eighteen birthday punches and one for good luck."

"Shadow could have gotten out."

Chris rolls his eyes. "I locked him in the bathroom." He places his large hands on each side of Scott's face as though he were about to pull him in for a kiss. "How are you?" he asks.

"I miss you. I'm sorry I—"

"I'm sorry, too. I should have stopped by but..."

"It's okay. I'm glad you're here."

Chris playfully slaps the side of Scott's face and then turns as Sarah walks out of the basement door carrying the plastic bin of discarded items.

"Did you know it was him?" Scott asks.

Sarah drops her smile into mock anger. "I expected something more original."

"I can't always be on my A-game," Chris says. He pulls out a six-pack of beer from one of two bags sitting on the kitchen table. "But I've already made it up to you."

"You know I don't like beer," Scott sighs.

"That's for me," he says, incredulously, and then points toward the other plastic bag. "A bottle of wine for Sarah and your gift are in that bag."

Chris walks over to Sarah and takes the bin from her. He slowly places it on the table, turns, and then opens his arms. Instead of a typical hug, he collides with her chest, knocking her backward, and then catches her body with both arms and pulls her into a tight embrace. His black skin makes her skin look paler than usual. They laugh as they hold each other.

Being together in one room again gives Scott a feeling of joy that he hasn't felt since his mother's death.

It won't last. Nothing good lasts. At least not for you.

"How you doing, buddy?" she says, her breath sucking in from being knocked out.

"Shitty," he says, releasing her with a smile.

Scott tries to pull apart the knot in the plastic bag as Chris walks into the hallway and opens the bathroom door. Shadow runs out and into the living room and is heard bounding up the steps into Scott's room.

"Is that why you already started drinking tonight?" Scott asks.

"You betcha," Chris says.

"What's wrong?" Sarah asks.

"Only call of the day we got went through cardiac arrest. He died while I was doing CPR. Didn't think I was such a bad kisser," he laughs while cracking open a beer.

Chris barely passed any of his junior year classes in high school, but aced every medical and physical test to become an EMT-in-training in his spare time. He is only riding secondary until he graduates, but he already is feeling the fallout of working with people in need. For him to be so affected by the lives he encounters while on the job without even being a full-time paid employee fills Scott with empathy. He does not want his best friend to give up on his one dream over outcomes he can't control.

"Can't save them all," Scott says, still struggling to untie the plastic handles.

"Sorry to hear that," Sarah says. She squeezes Chris's shoulder.

"Death one, Chris zero," he says as he swallows his first swig. He releases a fake burp as he takes the bag from Scott and rips it open. "What's with the Tupperware?"

"Clutter we're trying to get rid of," Sarah answers.

"Oh," Chris rubs his hands together. "A ritualistic burning?"

Scott ignores that idea because he hasn't decided to get rid of anything. He's also nervous that Chris is being literal about setting them on fire.

From the bag, Chris pulls out a hefty metal flashlight at least three feet long. "Water-resistant, full metal body, windshield punch on the back, and the light output is crazy. This thing will light up a room and beat anyone standing there to death."

"You got me a flashlight that can kill a man. That's very...you."

"Just looking out for ya', Scotty. I know how afraid of the dark you are."

"I'm not afraid of the dark."

"Cause you've always had me to protect you."

"You're the only one I ever need protection from."

"Well, with this, maybe you'll stand a chance."

"Good point," he laughs.

Chris' pudgy cheeks swell as he returns the smile. "Dinner's on me. DiNizo's?"

Scott tenses. He knows Chris is not trying to bait him into leaving and is only suggesting going out because his older brother manages the restaurant and lets him order drinks.

"Let's get it delivered," Sarah offers.

Chris nods. Sarah's prompting reminds him that his self-imposed isolation has caused a paradigm shift in their usual dynamic.

You are a disruption to their lives.

"Sounds good to me," Chris says. "What should I order?"

"Surprise us," Scott answers.

"Will do. Where's the Nintendo?"

"On the game shelf in the basement," he replies quizzically. "You want to play that?"

"It's been a while," he shrugs. "You're a man now. Let's say goodbye to youth in the best way possible. He pulls his cell phone from his pocket and walks into the hallway and through the basement door. His voice echoes as he orders food, and under his heavy stature, the sound of creaking steps rises as he descends the stairway.

Scott opens the refrigerator and places the six-pack inside. The thought of them playing video games together fills him with a little bit of comfort and excitement he has not felt in a while. He pushes the refrigerator door-

Don't trap that thought inside.

Scott catches the door from closing.

He imagines grabbing the thought and pulling it off the refrigerator shelf where he had placed the beer. If the thought gets trapped inside, it might not happen. The Nintendo will no longer work, or the power will go out. Something.

"Scott," Sarah says.

She's watching you.

"It's my turn to give you a present," she says.

He closes the door. The thought is still stuck inside, but he promises to rectify that later when he is alone.

Sarah sits at the kitchen table and pulls a wrapped box from her canvas bag.

"You didn't have to get me anything," he says while playfully snatching the box from her hands.

"Don't judge too harshly on the wrapping job. We ran out of wrapping paper, so I had to use construction paper from my old crafts desk and..."

He rips through the paper as greedily as a kid on Christmas. Underneath is a white clamshell box that looks like the kind that houses a wedding ring. His heart skips a beat at the minuscule chance of that happening.

Do you think she wants you to run away with her? That's hysterical.

Inside is an analog watch with a brushed-silver body and a glass face that shows the gold cogs of its inner workings. "This is gorgeous."

"I had it custom made. There are no numbers or arms."

"Okay, interesting. What does that mean?"

"I have my reasoning. You interpret it as you want."

"This must have been expensive, I don't deserve—"

"Stop," she says, sternly.

She knows you don't deserve it.

"That's really thoughtful. Thank you, Sarah." Does he hug her? Kiss her? Instead, he clasps the watch around his wrist. It's a perfect fit and feels heavy and solid.

"You're welcome," she says, and their eyes exchange equal amounts of affection and sorrow.

Chris returns from the basement and walks into the living room. Neither Scott nor Sarah pull their eyes from each other.

"Sarah, I don't know what to do."

"I don't know what you should do, either. I do know that I will be here to help." She reaches out and grabs his hand.

Until she is sick of you.

His body weakens under her touch. He wants to collapse into her, to have her cradle him, kiss him, tell him it will be all right and...

Nothing will ever be all right.

...tell him that he is forgiven.

"Why were you staring into the refrigerator for such a long time?" She looks more worried to have asked the question than curious about his answer.

His body stiffens.

She knows how crazy you've become. How crazy you've always been.

"Just... looking for a snack," he lies.

"Okay," she smiles. Scott can see the worry on her face, but before he can say anything, she walks away and into the living room.

Get used to watching her walk away.

Sarah lies on the couch and pulls a notebook and pen from her canvas bag while Chris finished plugging the Nintendo into the back of the TV. He hits the power button, and it turns on as though it was made yesterday instead of years ago. During their elementary and middle-school years, Chris would often get off at Scott's bus stop and the two would spend the afternoon playing together. If the weather wasn't favorable, video games would be the go-to. They'd lay on the floor and look up at the television, not blinking until the game was won, or Mom made them dinner.

Although Chris played sports games with his brother, he would choose a co-op game for him and Scott. Bubble Bobble or Double Dragon. Any game where they can fight together. He lies on the floor and picks out their favorite: Contra. He enters the classic Konami Code to gain an extra thirty lives because the game is a chaotic barrage of gunfire and enemies and they had never been able to beat it with the default three lives.

Chris selects two players and pushes start. A blue soldier and a red soldier somersault from the sky in eight-bit glory. They land on a grassy cliff overlooking a body of water. They are supposed to run to the right where they will be immediately confronted by an onslaught of alien foot-soldiers.

Scott had been sure that his friends showed up out of pity, but as they talked, as they laughed, he realized that nothing between them had changed.

Everything has changed. You just don't see it.

Scott pushes on the right arm of the D-pad and his avatar begins to run. Chris's soldier runs left and plummets off the cliff and into a pixelated, watery grave. He unleashes a boisterous laugh and rolls onto his side. His face is blood red, and he holds his stomach as though laughing is painful and what just happened is the funniest thing that has ever happened.

Scott rolls his eyes and drops the controller. "You really need to stop drinking."

His friend's idiocy is extra frustrating because it has been so nice to get back into their old routine. The simpatico of fighting alongside his friend, without the need for words or communication beyond their normal rhythm, would have been more relief than he has felt in months.

Never again.

"You need to start drinking more," Chris says through his maniacal laughter. "Maybe it will make you less crazy."

"Chris," Sarah says as she looks up from her notebook.

He ignores her and struggles to stand, knocking over the beer bottle and spilling it across the carpet. Scott picks it up and heads for the kitchen. Chris's laughter stops abruptly.

"I'm not done with that."

"Yes, you are," Scott says.

Chris follows him into the kitchen. "Dude, what's wrong with you?"

"What's wrong with me?" Scott throws the bottle into the garbage.

"What, because I'm buzzed?"

"No, because you're drunk."

"No, unfortunately, I'm not, but I'm getting there. I'll crash here if you want."

"Is that the only reason you're here? You just need a place to drink?"

You were a fool to think otherwise.

"Excuse me?" Chris seethes. His typically rouge skin darkens to crimson. Scott has seen him angry before - when he argues with his father or his brother - and his ferocity is frightening. Scott can feel the heat coming off of his friend and realizes that if he isn't careful, Chris will physically react.

"I forgot that it's all about you, Scotty. No one else can have problems because 'Scott needs us.'"

Scott knows he's quoting Sarah. Had they been getting together while he was stuck inside?

"What about me?" Chris asks.

"What do you mean?" Scott's anger rises.

Sarah enters the kitchen and leans against the wall. She and Chris exchange a look that Scott can easily see holds meaning that goes beyond that moment.

"What's going on?" he asks, looking solely at Sarah.

They lived on without you. Together.

Chris moves between them before she can speak and lifts the plastic bin from the table. He knocks shoulders with Sarah as he passes into the hallway.

"What are you doing?" Scott asks as he follows Chris down the hall and into the guest room, across from the master bedroom.

Chris slides the back door open and walks across the concrete slab that lines the in-ground pool. He stands at the edge of the water and pulls off the bin's lid.

"Chris, don't!" Sarah says as she steps outside. "He needs to be the one to get rid of it."

Chris turns the bin over and its contents splash into the water.

"You asshole!" Scott yells as he rushes to tackle his friend into the pool.

Chris is unmoved by the collision. He grabs Scott under the arms and lifts him into the air like he weighs nothing. He carries him across the concrete, through the tomato plants that line the house, and then pins him against the back of the house.

"What the hell is wrong with you?" Scott yells as he struggles to get free of Chris' grip.

Sarah hurries toward the pool and grabs at the floating papers and toys.

"Let it go, Sarah," Chris orders. He drops Scott, causing him to fall on his ass.

"That was a dick move." He is a foot taller than her, but that does not stop her from getting close to him. Even though her face is stoic, Scott knows her well enough to understand that her slightly furrowed brow and her ramrod shoulders mean that she is furious. "He's sick, and you're not helping."

Scott's stomach clenches. She thinks I'm sick?

She thinks you're a lunatic!

Chris stares down at her. Scott doesn't know if he is going to hit her or kiss her, and the prospect of either makes his stomach clench harder.

"Why don't you tell Scott why you're really here?"

Sarah's jaw clenches and her eyes burn with anger.

Scott holds his breath. His worst fear is about to become reality: she is there for one final night before telling him she does not want to see him again.

She threw you one last pity party!

She does not flinch as she stares up at Chris. He shakes his head and walks toward the gate that leads to the side porch.

"Chris," Scott calls after him as his friend opens the gate and lets it slam shut as he leaves.

"He'll come back," Sarah sighs.

An ambulance's siren screams, and with its blue and red lights it cuts through the late night, surely waking everyone on the cul-de-sac. The sound and lights paint the houses and trees until they diminish somewhere beyond the neighborhood.

"If he doesn't kill himself, first," Scott says.

Sarah sits cross-legged on the concrete in front of him.

"He's seen a lot of death," she says.

"And I haven't?" Scott snaps at her.

"No, you haven't," she answers sternly. "Not like he has."

"How can you say that?"

"Your mother died way before her time, and that feeling can't be matched. But everyone has battles to fight. You don't get to have a monopoly on grief."

Scott wants to scream at her, but he is accustomed to her always being smarter and more aware of people and their feelings.

"So, what do you have to tell me?" he asks. He smacks the back of his head against the house.

"I'd rather we talk about it later."

"That'll kill me," Scott says.

"I know..." she trails and then averts her eyes. "I'm graduating early. I've already been accepted to a school in upstate New York. I leave next month, and it's been eating me up that I haven't talked to you about it."

She's moving far away from you.

"Go home, Sarah," he says through clenched teeth.

"Do not talk to me like that."

"You said it yourself. I'm sick. Stay away from me in case I'm contagious."

"That's not what I meant."

"Does it matter? You're leaving. You don't have to deal with me any longer."

Sarah breathes in deeply and then slowly lets it out.

Scott looks up at the night sky, so he doesn't have to feel ashamed under her meditative gaze. A colony of bats flies across the full moon. Four, he counts. Four bats. Taking the time to count them calms his nerves. "I think I need to be alone for a little while," he says.

"Do you really need to be alone, or are you punishing me?"

"I'm punishing myself," he says. "I'll be fine. I'm just going to do some cleaning around the house. Clear my head."

"Okay," she stands.

"But if I change my mind..."

Sarah offers her hand to help him stand, and when he does, she does not let go. "You know where to find me," she says. She kisses him on his cheek and then moves across the yard toward the gate.

He looks away. He can't watch her leave. Not again. Not if it could be the last time.

Every time could be the last time when you're involved.

He walks toward the sliding door but stops before going inside. Since he's been forced outside, he might as well breathe in some of the night. Crickets chirp. Cicadas sing. Fireflies burst in and out of existence, and with them, he remembers a summer night of Sarah catching them in bottles while pleading with Chris not to tear their bulbs off.

The dirt that nourishes the tomato plants is fragrant and fresh. A section of the plot at the end of the house has been uprooted. His father must have started digging the bedding up so he could replace it with stone.

Another thing that's my fault, he thinks. They could keep his mother's tomatoes growing if he was strong enough to help.

If you weren't so sick in the head.

Scott walks into the house. The rhythmic sound of cicadas cuts off as he closes the door. He walks into the living room and collapses on the floor, aware for the first time that night that he is still in his pajamas and neither of his friends asked him to change.

They must think you're too far gone.

The smell of the spilled beer fills his nose and makes him nauseous, but he is too weak to turn his head. The chip-tune music of the video game is still playing as Scott screams into the carpet until his voice breaks and his mind threatens to do the same.

CHAPTER THREE

SCOTT LIES IN A fetal position, body still, throat silenced by exhaustive crying. He welcomes the feeling because if his body naturally shuts down he doesn't have to worry about reciting a plea for an uneventful sleep like most people count sheep.

Please no bad dreams, he recites in his mind.

Please no bad dreams, he repeats.

Please no dreams at all.

An hour or so later, he might be asleep.

There's always one option that will put you to sleep...

He pushes away the thought. He's not strong enough to go through with it, no matter how much the people around him will be better served with him finally out of their lives.

Maybe that's how you make amends? Finally, being strong enough to put others first?

He hasn't considered that, and it's sound logic...

A knock against the front door steals his attention. Sarah, possibly hearing his childlike tantrum as she made her way home.

You can't even suffer in silence. Wake the whole neighborhood with your pity party.

He stands and tries to see who the visitor is through the oval window in the door, but it is only the night sky. He wipes the tears from his face with the bottom of his shirt and unlocks the deadbolt. Shadow slithers between his ankles and hisses at the door.

"What's up with you?" Scott asks, reaching toward Shadow to drop him onto the couch. The cat twists out of his grasp and rakes his claws across Scott's forearm.

"Dammit! What the hell is wrong with you?"

Shadow runs into the hallway.

Scott opens the door and turns on the bright white porch light.

No one is standing there.

He hears a car's engine dying in the distance. He looks down to see a stack of two pizza boxes with the name "Dinizo's" written on top in bold, red letters. As he bends to pick them up Shadow yowls and runs between Scott's legs.

"Shadow!" he yells, and then steps onto the porch. The cat races across the street and into Mr. Shirley's unkempt lawn.

You just killed the only friend you have left.

He grabs his cell phone from the living room table and puts on his shoes. As he steps up to the open door, he stops as though an invisible barrier blocks his way.

Everything is fine, he thinks. This is your neighborhood, your home. You should not be afraid of your own home.

He takes in the view from his doorway. The lights from houses and street lamps hover like fireflies in the night. Moonlight highlights the greens of the lawns and trees and glistens off the street, tranquil and inviting. But there is a lot of darkness between those splashes of light, and no matter how well he knows the neighborhood, he can't help but be afraid of the spaces where he can't see.

You're still afraid of the dark? How old are you today?

Don't think. Just act. Get Shadow back into the house. Be there for the one life you are responsible for keeping alive.

You were responsible for your mother.

A rebellious scream helps him tear through the invisible barrier and onto the steps. He leaves the blanched porch light's reach and moves into the blue summer night. The sound of crickets and shaking leaves remind him of what he has been missing.

What you no longer deserve.

Mud and grass cake his shoes and soak the cuffs of his flannels as he follows Shadow through Mr. Shirley's front lawn.

Are you sure you won't make things worse than they—

Shadow slips between the gap in the steel gate that leads to the backyard. If Bastion is back there, Shadow doesn't stand a chance of survival. Scott concentrates on his destination while trying to ignore the darkness surrounding him. The fear of it chills his spine, but the fear of losing Shadow is greater.

As he crosses Mr. Shirley's lawn he sees that the gate is locked so he climbs over it, knowing he can from the amount of times he had done so as a child. The garden hose trips him up at the side of the house, but he keeps his footing and rounds the back corner and into the yard. He expects to see Bastion chained to his doghouse but the grass is so overgrown that only its white roof pokes through the canopy, reminding him of his neglect to fulfill his mowing duties and his father not having the time to do it in his absence.

Such a disappointment.

"Shadow!"

Moonlight highlights the edges of the grass and house, but is not strong enough for him to see the darker spaces. He moves cautiously forward, thick grass crunching beneath his shoes. The tops of the blades twitch as a pit bull grunts underneath. Scott has seen what the typically kind canine can do to squirrels, some of which had been the size of Shadow.

"Bastion," he calls with the high-pitched, light-hearted tone he used when he had walked the dog. "It's Scott. Don't freak out."

An aggressive bark rises from the grass.

Shadow hisses and screeches.

The grass rustles. A blur of black darts out of the grass, followed by a blur of white. They glide over the concrete patio and through the square flap at the bottom of the back door. Scott rushes toward it and finds it locked. He kneels on the concrete and lifts the rubber flap. No lights are on in the kitchen or the living room beyond it.

"Mr. Shirley," Scott yells inside. "I'm coming in!" He then whispers to himself, "Don't shoot me."

The old man had been an urban legend to Scott and his friends when they were children. Their resident Boo Radley. He only came out at night to pick up his mail, let his grass grow until it was noticeably unkempt, and never raked his leaves in the fall. He never appeared at any of the block parties, and his house was the only house that went dark on Halloween night. He owned an ancient boxer named Bastion that he kept chained up in the backyard that barked at all hours of the day and was eerily silent at night. All the kids avoided the house, except for Scott. On his thirteenth birthday, his father told him he had to start helping the old man with chores.

"He's scary," Scott had said.

"He's a good man, Scott," Dad corrected. "Just do what I ask."

His mother chimed in, "Or maybe you can tell your son why people think his neighbor is scary?"

Although Dad looked annoyed, he relented. "Mr. Shirley is a war veteran with PTSD. Do you know what that is?"

"It's when something so scary happens," his mother answered, "that it comes back to you like it's happening again in real life."

"Oh," Scott said, and then asked, "Is that why he yells really loud sometimes?"

"That's right. But he's not dangerous. He saved many lives, and when your dad and I first moved here, he and his wife helped us out with all the fixings in the house because we didn't have much money to pay for someone to fix it."

"Mr. Shirley is married? I've never seen her."

"She was sick for a long time," his mother sighed and looked down. "She passed away about six months ago. That's why we would like you to help with his chores, since he helped us when we needed it."

That's when Scott started mowing Mr. Shirley's lawn, raking his leaves, and shoveling snow. He also walked Bastion every few days who, in reality, is an obedient and affectionate dog. His "terrifying" barks and "skin-crawling" growls had been reserved solely for squirrels.

Scott crawls through the doggie-door. As his head and shoulders slide through, something wet seeps through his shirt on his shoulder. He cranes his neck to look at the flap resting on the back of his head and sees a smearing of blood.

You killed your cat.

Once his upper body is inside, the rest of him slides through easily and rolls into the middle of the kitchen floor. He stands and grabs the trash bin sitting next to the fridge and places it in front of the doggie door in case Shadow or Bastion gets past him and tries to run back out.

His mother's tomatoes sit in a dirty basket on a one-person table in the kitchen. He moves into the living room, where a low amount of light spills down the stairway from the second floor. The room is exactly how he remembers it: flower-printed wallpaper right out of the eighties, along with a shaggy carpet and furniture with enough torn edges and rusty brass that looked centuries older. A wood and glass gun-rack displayed various weaponry, dented and chipped so much that they must have come directly from the battlefield.

A dark stain on the carpet makes his stomach clench. He pushes the tip of his show on the area around the spot and sees liquid rise from the fibers. Fresh, and way too much. If this blood is Shadow's, he's probably already dead.

"Mr. Shirley?" He takes the stairs three at a time until he reaches the top. A moment of disorientation takes hold as he looks down a long hallway. Even though every house on the cul-de-sac is laid out the same, Scott's father had knocked out their hallway walls to make one bedroom when his parents decided they were not going to have another child. The kids in the neighborhood had been jealous.

"Mr. Shirley?" His voice echoes down the hallway. "It's Scott."

The passage is lit by a dome on the ceiling in the center of the hallway. A tulle veil of spider webs covers it and dims the sickly yellow light, just bright enough to catch the darker spots along the floor. He follows the bloody trail until he reaches the two adjacent doors at the end of the hallway. The door to the right is closed. He remembers it's a smaller room that Mr. Shirley used for storage, so he will be able to hear if someone is inside. The door to the master bedroom on the left is open. The bed's linens are untucked, and the nightstand holds a lamp, a clock, and bifocals on top of a paperback novel whose spine is too worn to read the title.

The bathroom light turns on and illuminates the bed. Running water and gurgling follow through the open door.

"Mr. Shirley?" He calls, moving further into the room until he sees the old man's backside hunching over the sink.

"Mr. Shirley," Scott says loud enough to overtake the running water.

The old man turns toward Scott and runs forward, barreling into his chest hard enough to knock the air out of his lungs and send him rolling across the bed. He gasps for air while trying to identify himself, but if the old man is having a PTSD episode pulling him out of it might be impossible. He's silhouetted by the bathroom light so Scott can't see if he is lucid. Instead of risking the chance he's not, Scott rolls off the bed and rushes toward the bathroom. He stumbles inside and slams the door, but there is no lock. He leans against it and catches his breath.

Mr. Shirley's body slams against the door so forcefully that Scott falls against the sink. He throws his hands up and uses the wall on either side of the mirror to brace himself before his head collides with the glass.

An acrid smell pulls his attention to the sink, where blood is splattered across the porcelain and surrounding a thick mound of dark red viscera lying inside. The center of the mass is lighter, almost purple, and pulsates as though something is moving around inside.

Another crash against the door opens it. Mr. Shirley bursts through. Scott turns around as the old man grabs him by the neck and squeezes.

"It's Scott..." he croaks as he tries to pull the hands from his neck.

A spot of blood flows out from between the old man's lips. His face looks like it has been nearly scratched off, with blood running between large bumps protruding from his skin like an aggressive affliction of poison ivy. As with the mound in the sink, a purplish tint is threaded through the wounds.

Rabies, he thinks. Bastion might have got it from a squirrel and attacked Mr. Shirley, triggering his PTSD.

The welts on the side of his face grow and the skin underneath bulges like there is something beneath that is trying to burst out. Scott scratches at his face, screaming as blood squirts from the wounds. He pushes Mr. Shirley toward the shower, tripping over the lip of the tub and falling inside. Scott runs out of the bathroom, through the bedroom, and into the hallway, closing the door to buy a few extra seconds.

"Mr. Shirley. It's Scott." Out of immediate danger, he cries as his mind catches up to what has transpired. "Scott Holland. I take the trash out, remember? You get me cool gifts for Christmas. Try to remember."

Scott is answered by the door slamming against his chest and sending him against the adjacent door. He turns to run down the hallway but stops as he sees Bastion standing at the top of the stairs. His lips are curled back, releasing a rolling growl from between bared teeth that drip with blood. The skin on his face is spotted with the same affliction as his master's, and a chunk of skin hangs from the side of his neck, exposing a part of his spine. Tiny purple veins stretch out from the wound and across his mug.

The dog bounds forward while barking frantically, blood from his wounds squirting across the fading wallpaper.

This is why you should never leave the house.

Scott turns to open the office door, but Mr. Shirley stumbles into the hallway and reaches out, catching him by the neck with a thick, calloused hand. He lifts Scott off the ground with such ease that it seems impossible even for a man of his build.

Scott digs his nails into the older man's hand and rakes his flesh, but Mr. Shirley shows no sign of pain. Scott's vision blackens around its circumference, but he still can see that the old man's eyes have changed. The whites of his eyeballs are bloodshot and a ring of dark purple circles his otherwise hazel irises. He tilts his head almost animal-like, regarding the younger man as though he has not known him for his entire life.

As Scott slips into unconsciousness, he sees Bastion calmly sitting at his master's feet.

Calmly. The dog doesn't have rabies. Nothing about this makes sense, but Scott is too tired to think straight. All he can think about is taking a nap.

Let it happen. Let the darkness drag you down. This is a blessing.

The prospect of sleep gives way to the need to stay awake. He lifts his legs and thrusts his heels into the man's chest. A sharp crack shakes the old man and throws him off-kilter, and lowers his arm. Scott finds his footing on the floor and tries to push away, but the grip around his throat hasn't loosened in the slightest.

Bastion barks wildly, saliva droplets flying through the air and across Scott's face. Nearing total blackout, Scott shoves his fingers between his neck and the old man's palm, scratching away at both of their skins until he has a solid grip around the base of the old man's fingers. He pulls back on them with his remaining energy until the fore and middle fingers pop out of their joints. The weakened grip allows him to pull away without taking off too much more skin. He shoves his weight against Mr. Shirley, and the old man's body topples back into his bedroom.

Scott reaches for the closed door and nearly faints as blood rushes back to his tingling head.

Bastion jumps toward him and clamps down on his forearm. He screams but uses the dog's motion to swing them around toward the bedroom. The dog's teeth scrape against the bones in Scott's arm before detaching. Bastion collides with Mr. Shirley as he moves to stand, sending them both across the bed.

Scott grabs the handle to close the bedroom door to buy him time. The pain in his chewed arm is excruciating, but adrenaline helps him push through. He runs into the storage space and locks the door behind him. Fists and claws attack the other side, so he pushes over a tall bookcase to collapse it and keep the door from opening.

The only escape from the room is a large window that faces the side of the house. He opens it and looks down at the concrete sidewalk and rusted chain fence. If he pushes off the house with enough force, he can make it to Sarah's lawn on the other side.

Movement from the adjacent window catches his attention. Sarah is standing in her bedroom, wrapping her wet hair in a bun with a small towel. A larger towel is wrapped around her chest and the water that drips down her skin glistens from the moonlight through the window. She is staring toward the side of the room Scott can't see, but he knows there is a large mirror with pictures taped around its wooden frame. Most of those pictures include him. At least they had the last time he saw them.

That's what you're thinking about right now?

A large chunk of the door splinters. Mr. Shirley's bloody hand spears through and pulls a chunk of it away.

Scott kicks out the screen and screams for Sarah, but the movement of her lips and a low rumbling from her house tells him she is blasting music. He waves his arms and hopes she turns and sees him. He looks around the room and grabs a book from the floor, but she turns from the window and out of view before he can throw it. He tries to throw it anyway, but the blood on his hands causes it to slip. It falls on top of the fence and is speared by one of the rusty pokes.

Well, you're screwed.

Bloody hands pull at the wood in the middle of the door until the opening is enough for Bastion to jump through. The wild dog lands on the downed bookshelf and bares its teeth. His hind legs bend, ready to pounce.

Scott throws his legs over the windowsill and plants his feet against the house. He looks down at the lawn on the other side of the fence and readies himself. Fear is keeping him still, but the heat of Bastion's smelly breath cascades across the back of his neck. He screams through the fear and pushes off the house, aiming for the lawn on the other side of the fence.

As gravity takes hold of his fate, he finds peace in knowing that if the fall kills him, it will be a quick death.

Chapter Four

A RASH OF VIOLENT coughs sends streams of blood across the grass. An object glistens within one of those dark pools. Scott tongues around his mouth until he finds an empty space, confirming that his single remaining wisdom tooth is the white object lying in the grass. His cheek on that side of his face is turning from numb to prickling.

A breeze stirs and reminds him he is out in the open. He turns onto his back and looks up at the window. His vision is blurry, but he can see that the space is void. He knows he has to move, to run for his life, but his body feels a thousand pounds heavier and his mind is reacting slower under the weight of fear.

He tries to stand, but pins and needles crawl through his leg muscles and force him to collapse. He feels a lump of pain on his thigh and reaches into his pocket to find his cell phone is cracked down the middle. He waits for the feeling in his legs to pass while keeping an eye on Mr. Shirley's back door. Half a nervous minute later, the sensation dissipates enough for him to move unsteadily across the line where the wild growth ends and Sarah's freshly cut lawn begins. His damaged vision pixelates the light from the lamp above her back door, but he does not need it to get into her house. Alfred the Gnome is the "keeper of the key," as Sarah told him when they were about six years old.

Scott tilts the ceramic ornament over and uses the key hiding underneath.

The door pops open and music assaults his ears. He stumbles inside and locks the door.

The song is blaring from the second floor. A woman's voice lamenting the death of a loved one, accompanied by soothing plucks from an acoustic guitar. A grungy, introspective, and haunting song. One of Sarah's favorites. Sarah's parents must be out, which means there isn't an adult to tell help him.

Didn't you become an adult today?

He follows the music into the hallway and through the living room, hunching below the windowsills to stay hidden. The pain threatens to collapse his body in that position, but he pushes through it and concentrates on reaching Sarah before he passes out. Not just for himself, but to warn her. He stumbles upstairs to find her bedroom door is closed. He uses his remaining strength to try to knock louder than the music and then rests his forehead against the door to wait for a reply. Pain and exhaustion threaten to take him under, and when he realizes she has not heard the knocking, he leans against the door and fights to stay awake.

"Sarah," he croaks as loud as his sore throat will allow.

The door opens, and he falls forward. He doesn't feel his body hit the floor, but finds himself lying on the carpet and staring at Sarah's feet. She screams, but it sounds miles away. The music stops.

"Don't move," he hears her say from that distant place. The frayed cloth of her white towel fills his vision and cold drops hit the side of his face. They are an oasis on his burning skin.

Sarah's blurry feet step back into the room. She kneels as she pinches her cell phone between her cheek and shoulder. Her other arm reaches out to place a hand on his head that he can't feel.

That doesn't matter, he thinks. He can rest. Sarah will save him.

His eyes lower along with his consciousness. He realizes with guilty pleasure that if he dies, the last thing he will see is her cleavage glistening with water instead of his face hitting the ground from two stories high.

You deserve the latter.

"What the hell happened to you?" Her voice draws closer.

It's okay, he thinks. I'll tell her about it all in the mor—

Scott opens his eyes. Adrenaline and fear lift his upper body and pushes the door shut.

"Lock it," he croaks, and then collapses.

"Hold on," she says, and opens the door again. He wants to protest, but sleep is too damn appealing…

A sting of pain opens his eyes.

Sarah is pulling a towel away from his face and dousing it with peroxide. She blots a few spots on his arms. He winces and then opens his eyes to find that he is sitting up and against her dresser.

"Sorry," she says.

"It's keeping me awake." He coughs through a nearly clogged throat. Sarah hands him a glass of water. The liquid bathes his tongue and tells him how dehydrated he is. The wonderful sensation brings tears to his eyes. He swallows it down until he feels something thick inside of his throat loosen and drop into his stomach.

A dried mound of blood.

She gently picks up his hand and blots the wounds on his knuckles. The white towel is stained pink. Scott realizes that at some point she had dried herself and changed into jeans and a t-shirt.

"Tell me you did not do this to yourself," she says. The drops of water on her face are tears. He hates himself for making her worry about him in that way.

"Mr. Shirley and Bastion have been infected with rabies or something that's making them act crazy. They tried to kill me."

"Mr. Shirley tried to kill you?" she repeats, rolling the words around her tongue and seeing how her brain reacts to the taste. She walks over to the window and opens the curtain. "I'm going to go lock the front—"

"No." He tries to sit up, but the pain in his side forces him back down. Sarah rushes back and gently pushes his shoulders to rest against the dresser.

"I don't know how much blood you have lost, or how deep your cuts are. We need to call an ambulance."

"We'll go lock the house first. I'm not leaving you alone."

"I can lock the house faster if I don't have to worry about you passing out again."

He sighed. "I think I'm okay."

Her face softens, and she nods.

Muscles ache and skin burns as she helps him up and then down the stairway. When they are downstairs, Sarah tells him to wait at the front door. She heads down a hallway, and then seconds later, returns with two iron firewood pokers from her hearth in the den.

"Don't be afraid to get stab-y," Scott rasps. The inside of his throat is hoarse and bloated.

"Stab an old man?"

"He's not the same old man. He's... ravenous."

"I'll lock the back and sides, you call..." she reaches into her back pocket. "Shit, I left my phone upstairs."

Glass shatters across the living room as Bastion jumps through the front window.

They scream and back away. Bile and blood fly with every bark as he turns toward them. Sarah grabs Scott around the waist and then opens the front door. She throws their collective weight onto the porch, and they stumble down the steps.

They trudge across the yard, but their bodies force them to stop and rest against the streetlamp against the side of the street. The incessant barking draws closer, and a breeze kicks up the grass, carrying an earthy smell laced with the stench of dried blood and body odor.

Bastion and Mr. Shirley exit the house and give chase across the yard.

Sarah tugs on Scott's waistband and pulls him across the street. He does the best he can to help her by pushing with his legs, but they are mostly numb. They reach the lamppost on the other side of the street. Another twenty feet across the sidewalk and Scott's lawn and they will be at his door.

Scott feels Sarah's grip loosen, and then the weight of her body is gone from his side. He hears the cling of the iron poker hit the asphalt before realizing his hands are empty.

"Scott!" Sarah screams.

Mr. Shirley is again holding him in the air by his neck. He kicks wildly at the old man's chest while Sarah whacks his arms with the poker. Mr. Shirley does not flinch, so she stabs the sharp end into his shoulder. His grip loosens, but still does not release. Scott scratches down the old man's diseased face, letting loose squirts of unnaturally colored blood and other viscous liquids.

Sarah swings at the old man's knee hard enough for it to crack. The kneecap dislodges, and it successfully buckles him over. The hand releases and Scott drops to his feet. He picks up the poker and lifts it over his head to bring down onto the old man's skull.

Bastion growls.

The entirety of the dog's weight crashes into his chest and knocks him to the ground. The poker skids across the blacktop and out of reach, so he pulls his knees to his chest and thrusts his legs forward with the little strength that remains. The kick hits the dog in his snout and tilts him onto his side, tumbling into the pool of yellow lamplight.

Scott keeps his legs up and prepares for another attack, but Bastion lets out a high-pitched whine and runs toward the far side of the light. Steam rises off the dog's fur, accompanied by the sound of a low sizzle like frying bacon. The smell is similar.

Fresh patches of discoloration boil on Bastion's hide. He licks the new wounds, whining in pain.

Scott uses the distraction to get to his feet. In the silhouette of the streetlamp, he can see Sarah kicking the air and fighting to break free from Mr. Shirley's grasp around her throat. He rushes to her aid, but Bastion stops licking his wounds and runs around the pool of light. Scott pivots to place Mr. Shirley between him and the dog. He grabs the old man's shirt and pulls hard, tilting away to utilize his weight.

Mr. Shirley's head tilts into the light, and the old man unleashes a guttural yell that also sounds like he has a throat filled with bile. He drops Sarah and stumbles into the center of the street.

Sarah collapses onto the asphalt. Scott wraps his arms around her torso to lift her, but she is limp in his arms. Her eyes are closed, but he can feel the warmth of her breath. He embraces her and stands while moving an arm under her legs to cradle her body. Although the pain is excruciating, he is able to carry her off the street and onto the sidewalk.

Bastion runs onto the lawn and blocks his escape.

The dog steps forward slowly, poised to attack. Scott takes a step backward, toward Mr. Shirley. He can't outrun either of them with her in his arms, so he turns his body so that he can keep Bastion in his peripheral view while addressing Mr. Shirley.

"Your name is Lionel Shirley. You have been my friend my entire life. You are a war hero, a loving husband, and a good man. If you're in there, please recognize me and let me go. My name is Scott Holland. I'm your friend."

The old man stops. He opens his mouth, but instead of speaking, he unleashes another liquid-covered grunt. He shakes his head violently and screams, then continues toward Scott with his hand reaching.

A siren screams through the night and diverts everyone's attention. An ambulance's headlights ignite as it rounds the corner of the cul-de-sac. Instead of shock or worry, Mr. Shirley turns back toward Scott and continues to cross the street.

The siren blares again, and still the man does not change course.

"He's attacking—" Scott tries to yell over the dying siren, but realizes it does not matter. The ambulance swerves toward the curb and collides into Mr. Shirley with a snap of cracking bones and bent steel. The vehicle pivots and hits the street pole, tilting it over and smashing the lamp.

Bastion barks and runs toward the ambulance to scrape his claws against the door.

Chris opens the window enough to talk through it without risk of getting clawed.

"Tell me I just ran over someone that needed running over," he yells over the snarling dog.

"It has rabies," is the quickest explanation Scott can offer.

"Oh, shit," Chris says, pulling his face from the window and further from Bastion's reach. The dog turns back toward Scott.

The engine dies, and the driver's door bursts open. It collides with Bastion's side and sends him tumbling over and back into the light. It yelps as its fur boils and sizzles. Chris jumps out and runs toward Scott and Sarah, placing one arm underneath Sarah's body to help hold her up.

"How hurt is she?" he asks without taking his eyes away from examining the wounds on Sarah's neck. Scott is unable to articulate a clear response. Chris must have seen something on his face because he grabs Scott under his chin with one hand and pulls his face closer.

"Jesus Christ, you're in shock."

Scott nods. "We have to get inside."

"I can't move her until you tell me what hap—", a screeching of metal draws their attention toward the ambulance. The front wheels lift off the street.

"Who the hell did I run over?"

Scott managed two words. "A monster."

"There's no such thing as monsters."

The old man tilts the ambulance up by its bumper as though it is not one hundred times heavier. The skin on one side of his face is mostly gone, showing torn and bloody muscle with a hint of bone beneath. One leg dangles as though it's dislodged from the hip. Shattered ribs poke through his torn shirt.

"I hope you're right."

The wayward leg pops back into place and the old man moves forward as if uninjured. He releases the ambulance. The front wheels crash onto the street and then bounce until it settles.

Bastion runs toward them.

Chris backs up while reaching both arms underneath Sarah. "Get the door."

Scott allows Chris to take her and then runs across the lawn and up the porch. Chris follows easily with Sarah in his arms and slams through the front door before Scott has time to push it completely open. Scott steps inside the house, but Mr. Shirley is already on the porch and grabbing at his shirt. He shoves his shoulder into Mr. Shirley's chest and the collision propels the old man down the steps and Scott into the living room. He hurries to his feet and grabs the door as Mr. Shirley slams against it with enough force to knock Scott onto his back. He stands quickly and pushes against the door while locking it.

The old man glares at him through the oval window, his strangely discolored eyes piercing through the dark. Scott notices the old man's eyes aren't wild or confused. They're angry, but still fixated in a way that says he's fully aware of his anger and in control of how he is using it.

He decided that he's the one who will bring you to justice.

No, Scott thinks. This is different. Those eyes no longer belong to the old man that lives across the street. Whatever disease he has, it has replaced his mind with something else.

Mr. Shirley backs away from the door. Scott moves over to the bay windows to watch as Mr. Shirley backs down the stairs and stops in the middle of the lawn. The disease spreads across his face and covers the open wound.

"Wake up, Sarah," Chris says, tapping the side of her face.

Scott takes his eyes off of the old man and kneels on the carpet next to his friends. He takes Sarah's hand and pleads to whoever might be listening to let her be okay, to let him be the one that gets punished. He deserves the pain, not Sarah. Whatever is happening, no matter how abnormal, can only be his fault.

You are Death.

CHAPTER FIVE

CHRIS KNEADS HIS LARGE fingers gently across Sarah's neck as she lies on the couch. Her eyes open as she draws in a breath that immediately turns into a cough, her skin turning from red to purple as she gasps for air. "Get her—" Chris says, but Scott is already moving into the other room to pour a glass of water. When he returns, Chris is holding her up in a sitting position.

Sarah gulps the water, coughs some more, and then finishes the glass. She clears her throat and breathes heavily as Chris continues his examination. He cradles her face in both of his hands and stares directly into her eyes.

Scott feels a cold sense of jealousy despite the terror of the moment. His two friends, so close, so intimate. Had something happened between—

She's almost dead because of you, and this is what you're thinking about?

"Can you talk?" Chris asks her.

"Yes," she winces. "Hurts like hell."

"Your neck's just strained. Nothing was crushed or broken."

"Thank you," she says without taking her eyes away.

Scott's jealousy strengthens.

You selfish asshole.

"No problem," Chris says. He stands and walks toward Scott, pulling down his collar to inspect him. His eyes widen when he sees the series of still-bleeding scratches stretching from the side of Scott's ribs to his hips. "Damn, Scotty. What did you do to piss off Shirley?"

"They have open wounds all across their skin with weird puss oozing out."

"Weird how?" Chris asks.

"Discolored," Scott continues. "Purple mixed inside the blood."

Chris furrows his brow in thought. "Could they have been poisoned? Touched something radioactive?"

"I didn't see anything," Scott says, "and Sarah lives closest to his house."

"I feel fine," her damaged voice says. "I mean, I don't feel radiated."

"Could it be some kind of rabies?" Scott asks.

Chris looks at him with a heavy amount of sarcasm in his face. "My uncle's Rottweiler had rabies. It made the dog violent and crazy. But it wouldn't have given' him the strength to survive getting hit by a van, lifting it off, and then healing a dislocated leg without touching it. Although..." he looks away, his brow furrowing again. "If whatever poisoned him destroyed his nervous system..." He grabs a few rags from the pile on the table and dabs at a few of the deeper claw marks.

Scott hisses in pain.

"Don't be a baby," Chris says.

"I'm starting to feel every single injury of the past hour."

"Yeah, that happens," Chris says. "Hold these against you. Keep pressure. Sarah, call nine-one-one."

"Don't have my cell," she says.

"Scott?"

"It's shattered. You?"

"Shit." Chris stands. "Mine's in the van." He looks down at Scott. "I'm going to run and get my phone and supplies."

"Wait," Sarah says.

"I'll be fine."

"We need to take a second and think about what's going on."

"It's fine. I'll be right back."

"Why did you come back?" Scott asks.

Chris looks down and smiles. "I didn't want us to go to bed angry."

"I appreciate that," Scott laughs.

"Look, I'll be quick."

"Chris, a crazy old man who might not be able to feel pain is trying to get inside and hurt us."

Chris shrugs. "I have to treat my friend's wounds when they get their asses kicked."

Scott lifts his middle finger. "I didn't know EMTs had an oath."

"Not as an EMT," he smiles, smugly. "As your stronger, cooler friend."

"I don't know if I should be honored or insulted."

"A little of both is good." He looks out of the bay window. "I don't see him or the dog." He moves toward the door and slowly opens it. He looks back at Sarah and Scott and then nods toward the bay windows. "Keep an eye on my back."

Sarah winces through pain as she climbs the sill and leans against the glass. The windows bow out, allowing her to see both sides of the house, the grass, street, and sky. Scott shambles across the room and holds the door open. His side throbs with pain from the few feet of movement, and he notices that he's left a trail of blood on the carpet.

"Bring back gauze," Scott whisper-yells to Chris.

Chris walks out of the door and briskly across the lawn, head darting, as he makes his way toward the ambulance. The door screeches like rusted metal as he pulls it open. He stops and looks around, but sees nothing. Sarah searches through the window for signs of movement. A few uneventful seconds pass, so Sarah nods at Chris. He climbs into the driver's seat, and a few seconds later his head pops out of the shattered window.

"Radio is busted," he whispers. He drops down again, and a second later appears with his cell illuminating his face. "The glass is shattered. I can't dial."

A shriek rings through the night. Chris looks around the truck, eyes wide.

"That didn't sound human," Sarah says.

"Chris!" Scott shouts through the open door as loud as he's able. "Come back!"

Sarah jumps off the sill and runs to Scott's side.

Another shriek, but lower in pitch. Another, and then another, all varied in their tone, volume, and length. Sarah looks over Scott's shoulder and says, "Doors." He looks at her quizzically then turns his attention back toward the neighborhood.

The doors of the houses around the neighborhood open.

Mrs. Campbell and her daughter exit the house and walk across their lawn. The same disease that afflicts Mr. Shirley now crawls across of their faces. They stare at Scott, transfixed, moving toward the house to meet Mr. Shirley, who has appeared on the lawn.

"What the hell..." Chris says. The color drains from his face.

"He's too old to be that quick," Scott says to Sarah. "Chris needs to get back here."

Sarah is looking from person to person as though she is searching for something.

"They don't care about him," Sarah says.

"What do you mean?" Scott asks.

"Chris is right there, but it's like they don't see him."

Scott stares into Mr. Shirley's eyes and the purple glow within. There is a pointed concentration in them. They register Scott's presence clearly, but without recognition. Not personal recognition, Scott thinks, but as though he is... prey.

No, not prey.

A target.

Sarah hurries back to the bay window and onto the sill.

"No, switch places with me," Scott says.

Sarah looks confused, but she complies. He braces his weak body against the wall until he reaches the windowsill. Sarah looks at him strangely as she passes.

Scott lifts himself onto the sill and nods outside.

"Holy shit," Sarah says.

The three diseased faces have turned their heads and eyes to stare directly at Scott.

"Scott, what—"

Scott yells, "Chris, now."

Chris pops out of the driver's open door and onto the asphalt. He weaves through the bodies who do not seem to care that he is there. He nearly tackles Sarah as he moves through the door and collapses on the couch.

"So," he says to Scott, panting to catch his breath. "What the hell makes you so special?"

Yeah, Scott, tell him.

Scott moves back to the door, and the attention of the three on the lawn follows.

"What are they waiting for?" Sarah asks.

Scott closes the door and locks it. He tries to connect the dots. Mr. Shirley is sick and crazy. Rabies? Medication problems? Chris mentioned poisoned. But who could have poisoned him, or the Campbells? As far as Scott knows, the only person to see Mr. Shirley that morning was...

Scott catches his breath.

"My father," he says.

"What?" Sarah asks.

"He poisoned Mr. Shirley and sent him to kill me."

"Your father would never—," Sarah says.

"Why not? His wife was killed. Who knows how anyone would react?"

"No," Chris stands. "Regardless, there are certain drugs that can make a person sick, crazy, or make a person do sick, crazy things through suggestion. For one to do all that at once?"

But then how could something like this be happening, specifically to you?

"Scott?" Sarah grabs his attention. "Are you with us?"

"They are acting crazy, and they are sick," Scott says, "but have the wherewithal to group up to stare at me through a window?" The thought of watching Night of the Living Dead with his mother last Halloween comes to mind.

And with that thought, a revelation.

It's the only logical explanation.

"They are coming for me, but not because of my father."

Whatever is happening to his neighbors, it is happening because of him, and the best thing he can do is give himself to the judgement that he knows is inevitable. Judgement he deserves.

The person he killed is here to get justice, possessing the bodies of his neighbors.

Open the door and welcome your mother home.

INTRUSION I

REMAINS

THE BOY SITS UP in bed and stares into the open walk-in closet where something has just whispered his name. The floor creaks as he steps down from the bed and reaches for his dirt-pocked hockey stick leaning against his bookshelf. He does not dare take his eyes from the space that he is almost positive he had closed before he fell asleep. He grips the stick with both hands, ready to beat back whatever it is that continues to whisper within. But what chance does he have against anything that lives in darkness? Not even the morning light coming through his bedroom window is strong enough to cut through.

The whispering grows louder with every step.

Scott

His body jumps at the call of his name. He shoves the stick forward and its blade is swallowed by the darkness. The wood stiffens and cracks.

Had he hit the whispering thing?

The stick gives resistance as he pulls. The blade is not covered in red blood or green ooze, but instead is caked with white powder.

His stomach clenches. He drops the stick and flips on the light switch. He is no longer afraid of the something imaginary, but something he caused.

Clothes hang around the space and pile on the floor. The only thing that should not be there is the crack he has made in the back wall.

The room spins.

His mother is going to kill him.

"Why the hell don't you think about these things?" His mother's voice echoes from beneath the closet floor. How did she know what he did already?

"I'm doing my best," replies a deeper voice.

The whispering was not from a thing at all. His parents were arguing. Again. As much as he wants to go back to bed, he knows he will need to intervene.

"Good morning, babe," his mother says as he enters the kitchen, her scrunched face lifting into a beaming smile.

"You're up early, my man." His father curls one side of his mouth and then takes a sip of his coffee to hide his lingering scowl.

"I heard you arguing," Scott says.

"We weren't arguing," his mother says with a laugh. "We were just having a discussion."

Scott nods his head and then opens the fridge to retrieve the milk.

"Don't spill that," his mother warns. "I just mopped the floor yesterday."

He nods again and then grabs and bowl and a box of Fruity Pebbles from a cabinet. He places them on the counter and pours the cereal. The colorful flakes ping against the bowl as he pours. He pops the milk and tips the bottle. Its weight is heavy, but he is confident that—

"Be careful," his mother yells.

Scott's body shakes from the sudden outburst. Milk splashes onto the counter.

"Dammit, Scott," his father seethes as he grabs a rag from the draining board by the sink and throws it over the spill.

"Mom scared me," Scott says.

"Don't talk back," his father replies.

"Sorry," Scott says.

"Don't say 'sorry,' just watch what you're doing."

Scott stops himself from apologizing again. He caps the milk and returns it to the fridge.

"That's all the milk you're going to use?" his mother asks.

Scott nods even though he did want more. He grabs a spoon and carries his bowl to the table. He crunches the dry cereal carefully with his head above the bowl to ensure that the little milk inside does not drip down his chin and onto the table. His parents just bought a glass covering to protect the wood and have stressed, at every dinner, their desire to keep it clear from stains.

"Anyway," his mother says to his father, "try to pay more attention to which card you use. We get a higher percentage of money back for gas and groceries on certain cards."

"It's hard to remember," his father sighs.

"But easy to remember everything you need for work?"

"Where do you think that money—"

Scott digs his spoon into the cereal to excavate for the red flakes before any other of the rainbow colors. The extra attention to eating them in a particular color order helps him drown out his parents' "discussion." He makes his way through the yellow and blues, and as he begins to scoop up the greens, there is a knock on the front door.

"I'll get it," his mother says, cutting off his father mid-sentence. Scott risks a glance toward his father, who does not show a change in expression as he takes another sip of coffee.

"Can Scott come out and play?"

Scott pops out of his chair and races into the living room. Chris smiles and waves at him from the open door. His pudgy face drops and nods as though he is too cool to show his excitement even at eleven years old.

"Did you clean your room last night like I asked?" his mother says.

"Of course," he replies.

"Of course? I never know with you."

Scott does not remember ever lying about cleaning his room - does not remember lying to her about anything - but is eager to get outside and play.

"I just have to clean up my breakfast." He tries to ensure that play time by being extra pleasant.

"I'll clean it up," his mother waves a hand in the air. "Get changed."

Scott races up the stairs to his room to change into jeans, a shirt, and his new fall jacket. When he returns, his mother's face contorts into disapproval.

"What?" he says.

"What, what?" his mother asks.

"You were making a face."

"No, I wasn't."

"Oh," is all Scott can say to that. "Can I go?"

"You're wearing your new jacket," Mom says.

He hears a hint of accusation in her voice. "Is that okay?"

"Yes, it's fine. Don't get it dirty." She turns around and points a finger in Chris's face. "And I don't want either of you going down into the well again. Hear me?"

Chris looks down as though he is ashamed, but Scott can see the smile he is hiding from her.

"I'll make sure they don't," a high-pitched voice rises from behind Chris. He moves to the side of the porch so that Sarah can be seen.

"Thank you, Sarah," his mother says.

Sarah beams with acceptance, knowing that she is trusted.

"You can trust me, too," Scott says, stomping the ground and pretending to whine.

"Scott," his father's stern voice calls from the kitchen.

"I was joking," Scott says, feigning a laugh.

A coffee cup clangs on a countertop and heavy feet creak across the floor.

"He was, Ed," his mother hurries to say. His father's footfalls cease. He looks at the floor to hide the heat that has reddened his face.

"Ready to go?" Sarah's sympathetic voice cuts through the heavy silence.

The well lies in the middle of the cul-de-sac, on a grassy island where the three children like to play. Scott takes a glance up toward his dirt-caked bedroom window and thinks he sees his mother's face making sure he does not go down. He has no desire to. It was smelly and dark and wet. He told her that.

"Quick, Scott. Enter the password to keep it sealed!" Chris runs up the grass.

Sarah looks at Scott sideways. They all know they are getting too old to play the same games, but still he yells, "On it," and runs to stand on the inlaid stone that was once a protruding well. A circular iron cover seals its mouth, carved with the word: KNOTS.

Scott does not know if KNOTS is the company that made the cap or the company that sealed up the well, but that did not matter in light of the truth that he and Chris decided years before:

KNOTS stands for "Kill Nothing Other Than Supervillains."

The organization disappeared under mysterious circum-stances a decade before; all their old forts were abandoned... including the prisons housing their most vile supervillains.

The prison below.

Scott places his feet together and then hops on the raised "N." Then, he hops to the side and lands on the "T." Back to the "N," over to "K," and then all the way across the word onto "S."

Are you sure you are doing it right?

The voice is a whisper dripping with sarcasm.

"I'm doing it right," Scott snaps.

"Did you put the password in wrong?" Chris asks.

"What?"

"You said you did it right."

"I thought you asked—"

No, I'm asking. Is that the right code?

Scott thinks. He places his feet together to try again. He hops on the "N..." but is "T" the letter that should come next? He made the game up, so how could it not be right? Still, something about touching the "T" next does not feel... pleasant.

Try a different letter.

Scott agrees. He bends his knees and thinks about hoping the other way to pounce on the "K," but that still feels... uncomfortable.

You're taking too long. Bounce on the N a few times to keep resetting the process.

Scott nods and raises his eyebrows. That feels like the right move.

He bounces on the "N" three times. He wants to switch to the "K," but his feet continue to pogo on the "N" over and over—

His body is pulled backwards, and he falls onto the grass.

"Let a professional do it," Chris says.

The voice screams in his head.

He'll ruin the code!

"Are you okay, Scott?" Sarah sees him wincing through pain.

"Yeah," he says and sits up.

Are you me? He thinks.

Of course, I'm you. I'm more you than you are you.

What do you mean? I'm me, and you're in my head. If you're not my thoughts, what are you?

What I am I? What you are You? Can you believe we are We, too?

"You okay?" Sarah asks.

"Just thinking," Scott lies. "Trying to remember the right way to do it."

Stop your friend before he puts in the wrong code.

"It's open," Chris says. He bends down and sticks two chubby fingers into one of the four empty notches around the cap. He only manages to lift the cover a few inches before it slams back down. The sound of metal on stone rings across the neighborhood. The three friends stand still and wide-eyed, waiting for a certain someone to run out of her house and send them home.

He must have entered the right code.

"Scotty, help," Chris says.

"I'm not going to get in trouble again."

"Not unless you tell."

"Stop, Chris," Sarah says.

"What?" Scott asks. "I'm not afraid."

"Come here," Sarah whispers and holds out a hand. He walks toward her and intertwines his fingers in hers. "Listen."

Although at first he only hears a few birds chirping, his attention focuses on two voices yelling so loudly that he can hear them through the walls of his house. He releases Sarah's hand and turns away. "They just have loud discus..." His voice strains.

"Forget it," Chris says as he walks in the direction of his house at the end of the street.

"Don't leave," Sarah says.

"I don't want to see Scott cry because his parents suck."

Scott wants to rage at his friend. His mother treats Chris like a son. How can he be so cold?

"He's just frustrated," Sarah says, "because he couldn't lift the lid himself."

He probably just wants to hang out with Sarah, anyway.

"I know," Scott says.

"It will pass," she says. "Want to go for a walk?"

I don't think you should.

"Why?" Scott asks.

"Cause I want to?" Sarah says.

If you don't touch the letters right, the walk won't be good. You'll say something wrong, trip her, or worse.

"Is it okay if I just hang out here for a little?" he asks her as he looks toward the well cap and considers the task at hand. "Alone?"

Sarah looks hurt, making Scott's heart skip a beat. He does not want to see her sad, but she does not know how important it is to complete the code, for her sake as well as his.

"Sure," she says, her voice strained. "Can I come back later?"

It's up to you to make sure there is a later.

"I... don't know." Scott says, waiting for the intruder into his thoughts to elaborate.

You still need to enter the password in the correct order.

"Okay," she says, her face full of hurt. She forces a smile at him before walking away.

Scott is left alone. Even the birds stopped chirping. The only sound he hears is the muffled argument emanating from inside of his house. He walks up to the cap and reads each letter carefully in order. His insides chill and goose bumps crawl across his skin.

Open your mind and let me guide you.

Scott places his feet together and waits for the instructions.

Jump on N.

He complies.

Now the K.

The O.

The S.

Back to K.

End on T and then jump back to your starting position.

He performs the motions perfectly. The string tied across his mind loosens and his stomach unclenches. He has not felt this... calm in a long time. He kneels and sticks his fingers into the notch and knows that he is strong enough to open the cap.

I know the codes to the world. The rituals. The protection spells.

A moment later, his front door bursts open.

"Scott!" His mother screams through a crimson face. "Get in here, now!"

I will help you.

His mother holds the door open as he walks back into the house. His father appears in front of him before Scott's eyes can adjust to the change in light. Heat explode across his mouth and then his body falls. He opens his eyes and finds himself on the floor with his father hovering above with the back of his hand raised.

"Your mother told you not to go down there!"

"I didn't," Scott cries.

"Your jacket is filthy," his mother laments. "Your brand-new jacket."

"Chris pushed me down. I wasn't—"

"Don't talk back to your mother!" The second slap is less painful under the numbness of the first.

Scott buries his face in his hands and screams into the carpet. "I did the code right!"

Did you? If you did it correctly, nothing bad like this should happen. Try again until it's fixed.

"I don't want to hear your excuses," his mother says. "Just go to your room."

He bursts to his feet and runs up the stairs. He jumps onto his bed and buries his body in the covers, where he cries for several minutes.

Scott

He sits up in bed and looks inside the closet.

What am I doing wrong?

Everything, apparently. Which means it's also up to you to fix it.

How do I do that?

If you have the power to break everything, you have to have the power to fix everything. Put in the code correctly.

He grabs the hockey stick from the floor and walks out of his room.

His parents stand on opposite sides of the living room, waving arms and pointing fingers furiously. He does not care to pay attention to whatever argument is so important that it keeps them from noticing him standing at the base of the stairs for over a minute.

"What do you think you're doing?" his mother gasps and holds a hand across her mouth as she stares at the hockey stick. He is ashamed that his mother thinks he will hurt her, but then smiles at the thought that he has the power to scare her.

The codes.

The codes.

His father turns and takes a step forward. Scott pivots towards the door and opens it before his father can close the space. He rushes out of the house and hears the footfalls of his parents following from behind. He quickens his journey across the street and through the green island. He lifts the blunt end of the stick and stabs it into one of the open notches.

The wood splinters as the cap pops upward. He uses the leverage to topple the iron over and onto the grass.

You did it!

"Scott!" his mother screams.

"Don't you dare," his father commands.

He places his feet together at the edge of the well and looks down into the darkness.

I told you, Scott. I know the codes to the world. The rituals. The protection spells. I will make sure you have the power to fix anything that is broken.

He bends his knees and then hops into the well, no longer worried if his jacket gets dirty.

Scott Holland now has the power to fix everything.

Chapter Six

"The bad man is going to get you."

The boy squeezes his mother's hand as she pulls him through the packed crowd with enough force to sting his shoulder. Carnival music plays in the distance and colorful lights twinkle in the evening sky. Every few seconds, a seat from one of the grownup rides swings above, throwing laughter and screams across the churchyard. He smiles from ear to ear and wonders if he will be big enough to ride that one when the carnival comes back next summer.

"Hurry," his mother says, "or you'll have to wait for the next ride."

The flow of bodies reminds him of swimming in the ocean during the summer before. He had drifted farther from the beach than he had ever been without meaning to. Something, maybe like the shark from that movie his father loves, tugged at his legs. It pulled him under the water and didn't release its grip. He took in mouthfuls of salty water before his mother pulled him back to the beach. His father later explained that what pulled him away is called an "undertow."

The boy never swam in the ocean again.

He wonders if there is such a force on land that can pull him away if he lets go of his mother's hand. If he releases his grip now, will he be washed away forever?

"Don't let go of my hand," his mother repeats, "or the bad man will snatch you up."

Is the bad man one of the people surrounding him? His mother never gave a description of the man, nor had she explained how he had acquired the job of hunting down disobedient children. The man must always be around, with how often his mother says he is watching. The playground, the mall, or sometimes just outside of the house while playing on the lawn, constantly watching for the boy to slip up and move from his mother's view. The boy obeys, not just because he is afraid of being taken, but because he loves his mother and does not want to disappoint her. Her disappointment would be worse than being taken away from her.

But if this man is so bad, why is he afraid of his mother? Is she really that strong? Did she have a magic power that kept him away? If she does have powers, why not use them all the time, even if he gets lost?

A thought occurs to him that he had never considered.

The boy loosens his grip and pulls away from his mother's hand.

Did his mother control the bad man?

The crowd pushes him forward and knocks him to the ground. Towering faces with wide smiles and long teeth stare down menacingly as they pass. Above these terrifying figures appear a familiar face. It reaches down from the sky with a large hand.

The bad man has come.

A STING OF PAIN forces Scott awake. He looks around the room from his position sitting against the front door. Through blurry vision, he sees Chris's large frame towering above. The side of his face burns.

"Did you just slap me?"

"I needed to make sure you don't have a concussion," Chris says, "and I need help sealing the house."

"We can pull all the furniture against the windows and doors." He becomes nauseous as the words leave his mouth, envisioning the destruction.

You've already damned everything else. Might as well destroy the house.

Although his mother has been dead for six months, he can't help feeling terrified of dirtying his mother's carpet even though it's already stained with blood. Had he dropped merely a splash of water on it his mother would have thrown a fit.

Pretty sure she can't 'throw a fit' greater than what's happening now.

He stands and looks through the oval window. Mr. Shirley and the Campbells scatter across the lawn, their familiar faces hidden under the affliction crawling across their skin. Bastion is no longer with them, which is somehow more unnerving.

"They're here for me."

Chris turns Scott around and pins him against the door. Spit flies from his mouth as he says, "Those are your neighbors, and they're sick. They don't know what they're doing."

Sarah places a hand on Chris's shoulder. "I get that you are scared, but let's all take a moment to think this through."

Scott is relieved. If she believes him, that means he is not crazy.

Chris shrugs off her hand. "You're buying into this?"

"It's strange that they are so fixated on him."

"I think," Scott says, "you both should sneak out the back while I distract them."

"I'm not leaving you," Chris says. "So, stop with that shit."

"Then I'll have to make the decision for the three of us." Scott turns around and grabs the doorknob. Air pops through as he opens the door, but then the knob jettisons from his grip and the door slams. Chris grabs Scott's shirt and turns him around.

"You do that again and I'll make sure you have a concussion," Chris seethes into Scott's ear. "I'll need the extra set of hands if we're going to get through this." Scott can feel the heat off his friend's face. Chris lets go and shifts his eyes past Scott to look out the window.

"What are they up to now?"

Karen and Elisa take off toward the house in different directions, leaving Mr. Shirley alone on the lawn. A moment later, the sound of banging and scratching comes from every side of the house.

"What are they looking for?" Chris asks. "A way to get in?"

The lights in the house die.

"Oh, shit," Chris says.

"They are diseased, but smart enough to cut power to the house." Sarah says.

"I guess so," Chris answers. Unlike Scott, Chris does not realize Sarah was not asking a question, but continuing to work through the situation.

"We need to get some light if we're going to fortify the house," he says.

"We have the flashlight you gave me and one that has a crank to power in emergencies, but it's old," Scott says. "There are some candles in the attic I can grab." He pushes off the door, but Chris steps forward to stop him.

Scott lifts his hands defensively. "You're right. I won't leave you if there's a way I can help you get out of here. I'm going to get the candles in the attic so we can at least see."

Chris backs away, allowing Scott to run into the kitchen to grab the flashlight and then walk up the stairs.

Moonlight shines through the window above his bed, bright enough to make out the edges of the open room. Unlike the other second floors on the cul-de-sac, there are no interior walls to make a hallway and separate rooms. His father had demolished them before Scott was born to give him extra space.

Books are stacked at each corner in various configurations; paperbacks by size and by color. The hardbacks on the shelves by author, except for the ones that belong to a series. He often changes his mind about which arrangement feels better. On top of the bookcase are toys and other collectibles that have sentimental value. A paper-folded dragon his father brought home from a business trip to New Orleans. The first Ghostbuster action figure he owned.

Other items, including the first novel he ever read, Jurassic Park. He had loved the movie so much he wanted to read the book, and that was his gateway to reading. Even though its spine is broken and the pages have yellowed, it stays on top as a reminder that books are always the best escape, especially now that he is too afraid to leave the house.

Clean shirts and pants are stretched on top of the dresser. He has room to place them inside, but he can never fold them perfectly, and even if he thinks he has folded them well, he doesn't know how to store them. Color? Occasion? Season? He has ripped band shirts that he should throw out but are associated with fun concert memories. They can go in the closet for storage or...

What about the closet?

He freezes; he forgot to check the closet when he entered the room.

The duct tape he uses to keep the folding door shut is peeling off. He smoothes it back down, but the glue has lost its strength. He grabs the roll of tape from the top of the bookcase and rips away a fresh piece to seal over a section of the gap between the door and the frame. He sets the tape back onto the bookshelf next to his analog stopwatch. Its hands rest at two minutes and forty seconds, the length of time it takes for him to become a coward.

He would wait until dark, turn off the lights, and open the closet door to stare at the darkness and force himself to look inside. Two minutes and forty seconds later, he would race out of the room and hurry down the stairs until he was in the living room, turning on every light he passed along the way.

You're eighteen years old and still afraid of the dark.

Scott shakes his head. He's not afraid of the dark, not really. He knows there is nothing in his closet. No ghosts. No ghouls. Nothing to jump out at him while he's sleeping. Still, he is compelled to seal it shut. He has just never been able to understand the nature of his fears. Even before his mother's death, he has felt afraid seemingly more than his peers at every age, and as they grew older and left those fears behind, his seemed to mature as well.

As a child, he was afraid of the dark as a concept, then he grew up to know that sometimes bad things or people can be hiding in the dark. Now, he sees darkness as a concept of the unknown. When he stares at the dark, he begs for whatever terrifying fate that could be waiting for him to go away.

At least my time has improved, he thinks.

Don't be proud of that. You've been trying for years.

He pulls the tiny rope that hangs from the ceiling. Two sets of stairs unfurl from the dark and hit the carpet. Dust rains along with the musty smell of mold and mildew. The wood steps creak loudly under his weight. On the top rung, he uses the flashlight to peek around before lifting himself through. He stands and bumps his head on the ceiling's support beams.

Looking around the space, he tells himself that he is an adult and should no longer be afraid, having once imagined the attic infested with mutated creepy-crawlies. Besides, there are real monsters outside.

The Christmas storage bins lie in the back corner, so he stays low and inches forward across the slats, struggling to keep his balance. He rummages through the holly-shaped candy dishes, tree-shaped cookie cutters, and porcelain cherubs until he finds the group of long, red candles. He sticks four of them in the waistline of his pajamas and places their crystal holders on one of the support beams.

He picks up the flashlight to scan over the other boxes and bags around the room with the hope of finding other provisions. The pale light glints off framed pictures of the family, a makeup chest, and more. His mother's collection of porcelain cherub angels huddled together, some cracked from being haphazardly dumped onto the floor. Their fractured bodies surround a wooden cigar box he does not recognize. He shuffles over to it and lifts the lid's tiny gold clasp.

Black and white and sepia toned pictures of elderly people he does not recognize. Newspaper clippings about a parade for veterans. A piece of composition paper with a list of names and numbers, his father's at the top. Stapled to it is a torn slice of paper that states "Two bedrooms, affordable" in sloppy handwriting. Paper-clipped to it is a yellowing photograph of the house, before his father built the garage. A similarly yellowing envelope lies underneath, with his address typed as the destination and the return from Daytona, Florida.

Inside is a post-it that reads, "In case you're missing me," stuck to a photograph. He peels the note and finds a black-and-white photograph of a nude woman. Her body is thin and angled, framed by flowing brown hair that stretches across sand on a beach. Her breast are large, her body smooth. Her smile is wide and eerily recognizable—

He slides the picture back into the envelope and tries not to acknowledge what he has seen.

These memories must belong to his father. Scott has not thought of the man as being sentimental in the least, but it would be ignorant to think of him as not having a universal human feeling. His father had a life with his mother way before he existed. For the first time since his mother's death, Scott realizes that his father's pain might be greater than his own.

Beneath the envelope is a series of wallet sized pictures of his own chubby baby-face. A tiny pink tongue pokes out from behind thin, smiling lips. Cheeks are puffy with joy and his wide, tiny eyes are full of the same.

The next image is of a blue backdrop and white floor, most likely from a photo studio. A tiny stain coated the plastic across the baby's face. He tries to wipe it off with his thumb, but the grime will not clear. He leans in closer and sees an almost duplicate image of the previous picture, but if there is a smile, it is hidden behind boils and scabs of diseased flesh.

He drops the frame, and then holds his hand to his mouth to stifle a scream. After the initial shock wears off, he shines the light onto the broken glass where a disease-free baby smiles. Had he just hallucinated?

Your mind is breaking.

No, it's not. He saw that picture. Even if it was in his head, the image was not his imagination. It was placed there.

Keep telling yourself that, maybe you'll eventually believe it.

He grabs the crystal candle holders and climbs down into his room. He lifts the stairs and they cascade upward, slamming shut.

"You okay?" Chris yells from the living room.

"Yeah," Scott calls. "I'll be down in a sec—"

The little amount of moonlight is cut from the room as something moves across the small window above his bed. The glass shatters as a blood-soaked hand punches through. It flings something into the room and then claws wildly. Scott drops the crystals, jumps on the bed, and beats the diseased, bleeding arm with the butt of the flashlight. The arm is noticeably skinnier than an adult. He looks through the window in time to see Elise fall from the window. The impact of her soft body on the brick porch below creates a sickening sound loud enough for him to hear from inside, two stories above.

An awful smell attacks his senses. He looks down at the thing Elise threw into the room and sees an amorphous shape. He picks up the flashlight and shines it on the mass, which sizzles under the light. It shines across ears, fur, and two green eyes.

Shadow.

The cat's body is torn apart. Limbs and insides barely connected.

"Oh, God," he says and feels bile rise in his throat.

If there is a God, He sure doesn't care about you.

Scott grabs a small cardboard box from under his bed and dumps out the CDs he had saved from his childhood and scoops up Shadow's remains with its flaps. He can't leave the window unguarded, so he looks around the room for something to place on the sill. On top of his dresser are four glass mugs that are carved to look like heroes and villains from a Batman movie. One of the movies had a fast-food promotion that offered them. His mother had taken him for breakfast every morning just so he could collect them.

He pulls the bed from the wall and stacks the glasses on the windowsill so that if something tries to come through, they will topple and shatter loud enough to alert them.

With the candles, the holders, and Shadow's remains, he leaves the room and returns to the living room where Chris and Sarah are lifting the television stand next to the television in the bay windows.

"Don't leave for that long," Sarah says.

He considers telling her what happened, but does not want to deepen the worry on her face. Instead, he opens the basement door and throws the box down.

That's how you treat what's left of your pet?

If they die, or the house gets destroyed, at least someone will find the remains below.

He uses matches from the utility drawer in the kitchen to light the candles. Chris and Sarah enter the room and to turn the table against the sliding glass door and pile the chairs on top. The smell of cinnamon fills the kitchen with memories of Christmas Eve. His mother would light them and tell him that they were for Santa to be able to see around the house. Sarah and Chris would come over and open presents his mother had bought for them, and they would watch movies until it was time for the kids to go home and get ready for Santa to deliver his presents. Sarah must be associating the scent as well because she turns her eyes to Scott to share the memory.

"They remind me of Mom," Chris says, breaking the silence, but does not grasp the implication behind his words that haunt Scott and Sarah.

Scott does not correct his friend. He understands the sentiment. Although his mother is the cause of his fear, he still has the urge to hold her hand.

CHAPTER SEVEN

TIME CAN ONLY BE measured by how low the candle wax has melted. Outside, the friends that have turned into fiends scramble around the house, scratching across the siding, scurrying across the roof. It reminds Scott of when he was twelve, hearing similar sounds through the wall next to his bed. Only a few inches of plaster separated his sleeping head from whatever was scratching on the other side. His father found him sleeping on the couch every morning for over a week, so he ripped through the plaster and discovered a family of raccoons.

"They're just trying to get out of the cold," his father explained. "They won't bother you."

Now, Scott lies on the same couch, hearing the same scratching, wanting his father to be there to prove to him that he had every right to be scared.

Some creatures want to drag you into the cold.

"Can't they just throw things through the window or set the house on fire?" Chris leans forward on the window's ledge and peers through the crack in the barrier.

"Try not to give them any ideas," Scott replies.

Sarah sits on the floor and rests her head against the couch. "If they could, they would have already."

Scott watches as the shadows from the candlelight darken the blistering cuts across her skin. Everyone is in pain because of him.

Every. Single. One.

"If we're not going out and they're not coming in, then what?" Chris asks.

"It might keep infecting people," Scott assumes.

"Then there is only one answer," Sarah sighs. "We try to escape and not worry about hurting them if we have to."

Scott laughs. "Says the pacifist."

"I'm practical."

"Your life wouldn't be at risk if I—"

Sarah raises her voice and leans forward. "We are not going to risk yours." She takes a breath and lowers her voice. "If our options are to let people die or to let you die, I'd rather risk myself to keep both of those from happening. I know I speak for Chris as well."

Chris nods without looking away from the outside. "I'd rather die trying to save all of us than choosing who I let die in my place."

Scott wants to argue, even though he understands the logic. Death is likely, but they can at least try to survive. "We will need something to give us an edge. Knives, other stuff from the kitchen, it's all we have in the house."

"Why not try getting into the garage?" Chris says. "There are a ton of tools in there. A nail gun, a chainsaw, other stuff that might up our chances. A shovel, metal piping, anything."

"Sounds great," Sarah says, "but we will need to go outside to get there."

Chris lowers his voice as though the creatures outside can hear him. "We can get onto the roof from the window upstairs and jump down."

Scott shakes his head and points toward the ceiling, where feet continue to tread.

"Right," Chris says, looking annoyed.

Sarah stands for the first time in an hour. Her sudden movement startles Scott. "What's wrong?"

"I'm hungry," she says as walks into the kitchen. Scott follows.

"Want anything?" he asks Chris. His friend shakes his head as he continues his vigil.

The fridge has retained some coldness despite the lack of power, so they pour milk over Fruity Pebbles. The kitchen table has been turned over and set against the glass doors, so they sit on the floor. They exchange slurps and the occasional glare, but her eyes are not the only set he feels watching him. He risks a look toward the top of the sliding glass doors and the window above the sink. Purple-hued pinpricks stare at him like he is a piece of meat.

"We have a lot to discuss when we get through this," Sarah says, pulling his attention away from the eyes. Her rainbow-filled spoon is steady in front of her smile.

"Yeah," Scott says, "a lot of weird shit has happened tonight."

She raises an eyebrow and tilts her head. "You know what I mean."

"If we get through this," he says.

"When," she corrects.

Scott feels a vibration in his bottom.

"Did you feel that?" Sarah asks.

Chris says as he rushes into the room. "Did you feel that?"

They are answered by a large thrust against the floor.

Chris jumps and backs up to the wall. "Is the basement not locked?"

Scott thinks about the shutter doors that lead from the basement to the backyard. He knows they are always locked and his father never uses them. Scott lifts himself over the sink and peers through the window above it. He can see the bottom of the closed shutter doors below. How could something get in?

Another crash against the floor shakes the house and sends the three toppling against the wall. Whatever is in the basement must have already—

Then he remembers Bastion, the disease infecting him, and how the same disease stitched Mr. Shirley's wounded skin together and popped his dislodged leg back into place.

"Grab what you can," he says. "If you want to fight, we're going to have to start now."

"What is it?" she asks.

The thing in the basement slams against the floor again. They stick to the wall to keep from losing balance. Scott grabs a knife from the kitchen block shoved into the makeshift barrier.

"It's Shadow."

Sarah and Chris take this information in and then move with purpose. Sarah pulls two chopping knives from a kitchen drawer. Chris grabs one of the kitchen table's legs and strains against the weight of the thick oak until he pulls it into the hallway and rests it against the basement door. The legs are long enough that their feet almost touch the adjacent wall, a perfect fit to keep the door from opening more than a few inches.

Sarah hands him one of her knives. They wait in the hallway as the stairs below creak and snap, until a low, rolling growl lies on the other side of the door. Scott squeezes the knife's handle and lifts his other hand up to block whatever is coming. The growl grows louder until it snowballs into a deep roar.

All three take a step backward.

The door's upper hinge bursts from the frame and stabs into the adjacent wall an inch away from Chris' face. Another collision sends splintered wood in both directions down the hallway. The top of the door bows inward from the weight of a large, mangled paw. It reaches from the opening and brandishes scythe-like nails. They slice through the air, forcing Sarah to dive into the kitchen and the other two down the opposite end of the hall.

The paw retracts into the opening and is replaced by a set of green eyes. Scott is mesmerized by those eyes, because although they look hungry and ready to kill him, they still resemble the eyes of his friend. The friend that Scott cared for and petted, who sat on his lap and brought him string so they could play together. The friend who snuggled him at night and woke him from nightmares. The friend his father brought home to protect him from the raccoons in his walls and give him courage to go back to sleeping in his own bed.

The eyes retreat into the dark. The stairs creak, and then nails tap along the concrete below.

Tap, tap, tap. Then, silence.

The floor bursts upward. Scott and Chris are blown back against the wall hard enough to knock them onto the floor. The oversized paw with machete-like nails reaches through the torn carpet and swats around like the cat it used to be when reaching for a mouse under the refrigerator. Scott rolls away before a nail slices his stomach open.

Chris screams.

Scott sees one of the creature's nails embedded into his friend's thigh. It pulls him toward the hole as he rakes his fingers across the carpet for some purchase. Failing, he bends over and wraps two hands around the nail and pulls. Scott moves to the edge of the hole, lifts his leg, and smashes his heel down at the base of the nail at the toe. Fissures form through it like cracked glass, but stays intact. A deafening roar fills the hallway.

The paw lifts into the air with Chris hanging from its claw and slams downward. The carpet's tear widens as the flooring underneath gives way, and the claw drags Chris down. Scott tries to throw himself away from the hole, but there is no longer a floor to stand on.

A momentary veil of darkness blinds him as he falls and his back collides onto the basement's concrete floor. Pain shoots through his spine and air evacuates his lungs. Panic sets in as he realizes he is unable to move his body, but passes when his lung involuntarily gasps for air. He rolls into a fetal position and coughs until he can clearly breathe.

Black fur brushes his cheek. He lifts his head and sees Shadow - the creature he has become - is curled around one of the support posts underneath the stairs. He shuffles backward and stumbles as his feet, backing up to the farthest wall without taking his eyes off the creature. Most of its fur is matted with blood. Sections of the spine stab out of the skin like spikes. Blood trickles from those wounds, crimson with highlights of purple.

The creature turns its head to face Scott. Specks of the previous green eyes are scattered around the same purple hue as the diseased people. Those eyes recognize him, not as a friend, but a hungry lion stalking a gazelle.

"Get the fuck off me!" Chris screams from behind the creature. Scott can't see him but is relieved to at least hear that his friend is still alive.

The creature flicks its arm. Chris's body slides across the room and crashes into one of the wooden shelves against the wall, cutting off his screaming. Cans of coffee, soup, and other non-perishables fall on top of him.

"Chris!"

The creature stands on all fours. Its claws scratch across the concrete as it turns its body toward Scott. It is almost as tall as he is and twice as long as it used to be. The fur around its toes is mostly gone and the surrounding skin is shredded. Dagger-like fangs protrude from the skin around its muzzle. Purple mucus threads across the wounds and pulsates like it is alive. The disease looks as though it has molded around the muscles and spread them and its bones apart to give it more mass and deadlier means.

Scott spies the concrete steps, but he knows he won't be able to climb them and get the door unlocked before the creature reaches him.

One of its paws lifts off the concrete.

Having played with the cat for over a decade, Scott knows what is about to happen. He dives forward as the creature leaps, rolling under its body and narrowly missing being crushed under its weight. He uses the momentum to push onto his feet and slide between the sloping stairs and the water heater to get to Chris on the other side of the room.

His eyes are closed, and his body is still, but dust is blowing away from his lips from the floor. There is no way of telling how much he is hurt, but he is alive.

"Get up buddy," Scott says, tapping his friend's cheek. Chris moans.

The creature slips through the narrow space under the stairs. Scott steps away from Chris and places his back against the farthest wall. As he suspects, the creature ignores Chris and keeps its eyes on him. It lets out another high-pitched roar, a bastardized version of his former cat's meow. The sound bounces off the walls and stings his ears. He winces, but fights to keep his eyes open and attention forward.

The creature leaps from across the room.

Scott pushes off the wall and rolls forward, but the move does not work a second time. Its paw swats downward and rakes across Scott's leg. He screams as one of its nails slices through his jeans and across his flesh. The concrete batters his body as he rolls across the floor and collides with the shelving he had pulled off Chris.

The creature crashes into the wall. The foundation quakes. Its body falls to the floor and leaves behind a web of cracks in the wall that spreads and connects to the others that have formed over time. A chunk of concrete loosens and shatters when it hits the creature's exposed spine. A weak stream of water leaks into the room from the sewer behind the wall.

The creature stands.

Scott runs toward the stairs and ascends, desperately keeping distance between it and Chris but also wanting to be out of the basement's confining space. He keeps the creature in his peripherals as he ascends, expecting to have time to reach the door as it rounds the steps. The creature must have the same instinct because it pivots toward the side of the staircase.

It leaps and curls its body while it is in the air, creating a wrecking ball to smash against the stairway's support legs. The wood snaps in several places. Scott holds the railing as the middle section of the stairway drops and crushes the creature beneath. The sound of snapping wood is joined by the snapping of bone.

He grabs a piece of the railing that is still connected to the top floor to lift himself over the newly made gap, but notices a heavy amount of blood spreading across the floor from underneath the creature's unflinching body.

Scott drops onto the floor and returns to Chris. "Wake up," he says and taps on his cheek again.

The creature lifts its head, trying to shake the debris off its back. It reaches one paw forward, brandishing its nails and slamming the ground. Two nails crack the concrete and help it pull forward. One of the stairway's broken posts is sticking into its belly and emerging out of its back. The spine is shattered. The creature roars as it continues to pull itself forward, despite its skin tearing apart. Blood and purple viscera pour from the wounds as the upper half of hits body detaches from the lower.

The evil hunger in its eyes grows as it uses its other set of claws to stake the ground and thrust its upper half into the air. It lands with a wet slap a few feet in front of Scott and then reaches out with an extended claw. Scott leans back until the claw retracts, and the paw lowers to rest on the concrete.

Scott picks up a piece of splintered wood and lifts it above his head. The creature opens its mouth, but instead of unleashing a roar, it releases the mew of a much smaller cat. The tendrils of disease that tore it apart and held it together loosens and drips to the floor. The creature lying in front of him is reverting back to its original shape, but no longer able to keep itself together.

The cat's mangled, pain-filled eyes look up at his owner.

"I'm so sorry," Scott cries.

Shadow answers with a weak meow and stares at Scott with pain and confusion.

He wants to know why his father is not helping to take the pain away.

Scott does not have an answer, but a question of his own.

How many more lives will be taken in place of his own?

Chapter Eight

Scott dumps a shoebox full of photographs and uses it to scoop up both halves of Shadow's body. Although the disease still lies at the edges of his wounds, the cat's dead eyes have lost their purple hue and have reverted to their normal green. He forces himself to stare into them until he places the lid on the box.

The water seeping through the wall has reached the center of the room and soaks his shoes. The concrete is thinner because of the foundation butting up against the drainage sewer on the other side. If it rains, the basement will flood instead of the retention pond a mile away from the neighborhood.

The fun just keeps amping up, eh Scotty?

"Back away from the opening," Sarah says, and is heard moving around something heavy. A moment later, the table that they used to try to block the door slides down from the hole and hits the bottom, making a ramp.

Scott helps Chris over to the ramp. Sarah reaches from the top with a blanket for him to grab. His fist shakes and then releases the fabric.

"It's okay," Scott says. "I'll help you." He lifts onto the tips of his toes and hands the bloody shoebox to Sarah. He wraps one arm around Chris's waist and pulls on the blanket with his other to pull them up.

"Romantic," Chris mumbles, his head resting on Scott's shoulder.

"That's the spirit," Scott says. "Keep pretending you're funny."

Chris tries to laugh, but winces.

Sarah wraps her arms around Chris and lifts him into the hallway. When Scott comes out, they move Chris into the living room and lay him on the floor. His jeans are soaked with blood at his thigh where the nail had penetrated.

"Bandages and alcohol," Chris tells them.

"Medicinal or other?" Scott says, half joking.

"Both," he groans and then closes his eyes. Scott doesn't know if he should keep Chris awake, and only Chris would know if that's the correct procedure.

"I think I know what everyone sick's with," Chris mumbles.

Scott and Sarah look at each other and then wait for Chris to explain, but his heavy breathing develops into a snore.

"Chris," Scott yells and lightly kicks his friend's shoe.

Chris grunts and opens his eyes. "How long was I out?"

"Eight seconds," Scott answers. "What do you mean you know 'what everyone's sick with'?"

"Oh," his eyes widen. "Let me clean this cut while I tell you."

Scott hurries to the bathroom and sees the towel he draped over the window that morning. A flash of his baby picture with the disease crosses his face comes to mind.

Is that what you think you'll see on the other side?

He ignores the thought and grabs the bandages and rubbing alcohol from under the sink. He returns to the living room to find Sarah cradling Chris, as he had done for her only an hour before. Seeing them like that ignites a fire of jealousy in Scott's paranoid head, and he wonders again if something between them developed while he was stuck in the house.

It's not paranoia if it's true.

Chris rolls up his pants and pours the alcohol over the deep cut in his thigh. He tries to hold back from screaming, creating a sound more akin to a grunt. When the pain passes, he nods toward the shoebox.

"Open the lid."

Sarah does then turns her face away and buries her nose in Chris's shoulder.

Scott looks up toward the by window where purple eyes continue to stare at him from between the makeshift barrier. Mis-colored fireflies darting through the summer night.

"Look at the purple shit in the center," Chris says. "The afflicted are spotted with sores, necrosis, open wounds, and have purplish skin lesions. This looks like Porphyria."

Scott and Sarah look at each other.

"I know, I'm an idiot," he scowls, "but I've been learning about medicine since I was ten. Cut me some slack."

Scott stares at the floor and Sarah's face turns red.

"It's contacted through the air, touch, saliva, and can be passed from one of the parents. Rare, but it has happened. You never heard of it because we developed a bunch of medicine to nearly eradicate it. For people to get infected with it like this—

"Can the disease do that?" Sarah nods toward the torn remains.

A tendril from a section of the purple mass around the back half of Shadow's waist grows toward the other half of the body and is met with another reaching tendril. They intertwine and begin to pull both halves together.

"It's pulling the body back together," Scott says.

"Does anything irritate it?" Sarah asks, as though she has thought of something new.

Chris thinks. "People with it can't wear certain jewelry because of the metals it's made of... um... usually silver. Some oils in lotions. Sensitivity to sunlight is a big one."

Sarah looks at Scott.

"What?" he says.

"Grab a candle," she says.

Scott looks confused but decides not to protest. He grabs a candle from the windowsill and hands it to Sarah. She tips the flame close to the body. She moves away from Chris to lower the flame until it is almost touching the tendrils. They singe as though they are actively burning until there is nothing left. "I can leave this flame the same distance away from my arm and maybe singe a hair or two. This stuff is melting like it's on fire, but I don't think it's the heat. I think it's the light."

"What makes you think that?" Scott asks.

"You saw what happened to them under the lamplight. Their skin burned just as quickly. Out of the three of us, I figured you would be the first one to see the similarities."

"What similarities?"

"Your father raised you on horror movies."

He looks quizzically at her. What would he know about diseases, metals, oils, and people burning up under light—

"No way," his eyes widen.

Sarah nods.

"Okay, I'm back to idiot mode," Chris says.

"They're vampires," Scott says.

"Why? Because they have a disease that gets irritated under light?"

"It makes sense," Sarah says. "When plagues were rampant in the eighteen-hundreds, they did not have science to make sense of it, so they treated it like everything else they did not understand, with religion and superstition. Priests used holy water scented with oils, so when the sick started burning as they were being blessed, the church figured they were possessed by an evil spirit. So then, priests used crucifixes made of silver which burned them to the touch." She turns toward Chris. "I'm guessing garlic makes the disease worse, too?"

Chris nods. "It's an irritant, like metal."

"They also tried to treat it by having the afflicted drink human blood, thinking that it could replenish the blood lost through their sores."

"Drinking blood will mess with a person's head," Chris agrees. "But again, it's a disease. They haven't tried to drink our blood," Chris says. "Vampires aren't real."

"So, it's the disease the superstitions are based on."

"Vampires have no reflection in a mirror," Scott says, "which comes from the fact that those with the disease would cover up their mirrors so they wouldn't have to look at themselves. Mr. Shirley has a reflection. These things also don't care about being invited in. Where does that come from?"

"There is a bunch of stuff associated with the disease and mental..." she trails off.

"What?" Scott asks.

Sarah shakes her head. "Nothing. Nothing that will help. Vampires need to be invited in because people were so afraid of spreading the disease that no one was allowed into the household unless they lived there. But these things can get inside, so that's also just superstition.

"So, what does this mean?" Chris asks. "Create a giant spotlight from flashlights? Wear some of Mom's silver jewelry like armor?"

Scott leans against the refrigerator and stares up at the ceiling. "Mr. Shirley gets this disease. Shadow senses it, or smells it, and goes after him. Mr. Shirley attacks me, and when I escape, he infects the others. How? Biting them? And how did he get a rare disease in the first place?"

"We still have not considered the scariest part." Sarah adds then looks at Scott. "How can a disease convince someone to attack you?"

"Us," Chris says.

"You were out there in the middle of them, and they didn't care," Scott reminds him. "Mr. Shirley only went through Sarah to get to me. If this is a disease that can think, then why not go off and infect everyone it can? Why are they standing on the front lawn waiting for me to come out? Why is a disease after me?"

No one has an answer.

As Scott's question lingers, Sarah's breathing grows louder. Tears fall from her eyes as she leans against the counter and holds onto its lip. "You were right," she says. Her voice cracks as she looks at Scott. "This is because of your mother."

"That's ridiculous," Chris rages. Sarah's body jumps under his sudden outburst. "Even if supernatural crap is real, your mother would never hurt you."

"What else can this be?" Scott's voice cracks as well. If Sarah has also come to this conclusion, then his fears are confirmed.

"Even if your mother sent a deadly disease to kill you, I don't give a fuck. I just give a fuck about surviving. All of us surviving." He squeezes his hands together and steps forward. Scott braces for a punch. Instead, Chris lifts his finger and points at him. "I care about you surviving."

Scott swallows back a well of emotion in order to speak clearly. "I don't think I deserve that, but if I can help you out of this, you can count on me."

Chris's expression changes into contemplative. "I think our luck is already changing."

"How so?"

Chris unleashes a belch that lasts for a few seconds.

"I ate some garlic bread earlier," he says, forcing a smile.

"That's disgusting," Scott says, weakly returning the smile.

"But useful," Chris corrects.

"We only have the flashlight you gave me," Scott says, "and the utility one under the sink. But yeah, I'd put whatever we think would help around every entrance. Silver, garlic, candles, anything."

"What about torches? Grab some matches and—"

A muffled scream enters from the front of the house.

"That was definitely human," Chris says.

Scott and Sarah look through the oval window in the front door. Chris struggles to stand and then limps to the bay window.

The creature that is the former Mr. Shirley stands in the center of the lawn with Bastion sitting at his feet. The old, infected man holds David Miller in the air by his neck. The boy screams and kicks in the air, but his ten-year-old legs can't reach far enough back to hit the infected man. Karen and Elise Campbell flank each side of the group, now joined by Karen's wife Elizabeth, whom Scott assumes had arrived home to see her family changed.

Another scream cuts through the night.

Dan Miller moves up the lawn while dragging Nancy by her wrists. Her feet rake the grass as she kicks and screams against her husband's grasp. He grabs the back of her neck and forces her to kneel. His diseased face shows no emotion.

"They told me they will let us go if you come out," she struggles to yell through her crying.

"Of course," Scott says. He pushes off the door and leans against the far wall. He yells as he shoves his shoulder into it. The wallpaper rips and the plaster cracks.

Sarah places her shaking hands up to her face. "We have to stop this."

Scott turns toward her. "Just say the word and I'll walk out."

"Do something that doesn't involve giving up," she snaps.

He looks away from her disapproval. "If I go outside, everyone will be saved."

"We don't know that for sure," Chris says.

"No, we don't," Sarah says. Her face is red and her eyes stare daggers at Scott.

Displaying physical anger is so rare that Scott can't look away. "The only thing that seems to be true is that every time I have stepped outside of this house, something bad happens. What if Chris is right, and this is not just about me?"

"Pick one," Sarah says, her anger growing. "Is this all about you, or is none of it about you? It can't be both. Make a fucking decision. Do nothing or do something."

"But what if—"

"No," she yells high enough for it to turn into a scream. "No 'buts.' No 'what-ifs.' If you do nothing, nothing changes. If you do something—"

You will make it—

"I will make it worse," Scott screams.

Sarah steps away from his anger, then returns her own. "You don't leave the house because you can make bad things happen just by your magical presence? What makes you so special?"

"I never said I was, Sarah." His anger toward her is rising to an unprecedented high. "I killed my mother, Sarah."

"You do not have to punish yourself because you chose to do something that would make you happy. You went to the movies and your paranoid mother drove around to find you and ended up in a car crash. It was her choice. There was nothing you could have done."

"Exactly," he yells. "There was nothing I could have done."

Except for staying home in the first place.

Sarah opens her mouth to speak, but then stays silent. Her expression changes from anger to remorse. "You know, Scott, you might be right. Hell, there are literal monsters outside, so maybe you are magically the cause of it. If all of this is happening because at one point in your life you chose to do something for yourself, then it is logical that doing nothing is the better decision. But, following the same logic, doing nothing will not change what you already set in motion by doing nothing. Only doing something will change that."

"I don't think I have the power to stop this."

"Then you didn't have the power to create it, either."

Scott's anger fades. "I don't know what to do, Sarah."

"Let me make your decision easier, Scott." She steps toward him and cradles his face in her hands. "Someone's mother is about to die. Do something."

"I have an idea," Chris says proudly. They turn to look at him. He nods at the crack Scott made in the wall. He lowers his voice and glances outside as though he does not want their attackers to hear. "We can get into the garage through the wall in the master bedroom."

"You're just full of surprises today," Scott says.

"I think it's the impending doom."

"That checks out," Sarah says.

Scott looks at both of their faces, thinking about the times they were in this room as children, playing games and laughing.

And now you're the cause of their torture and death.

Scott nods toward his friends, to himself. He grabs the candle from the floor and holds it against Shadow's body until the fur catches the flame. The cat's remains, along with the disease, burns away.

He walks across the room and opens the front door.

The cries from Nancy and David sting his heart and clench his stomach. He feels the urge to run outside and give himself up to stop their terror. Sarah must have felt the urge in him as well, because she grabs the waist of his flannel to ensure he doesn't run.

The infected inch forward. Diseased faces of the Millers and the Campbells of Village Court. Only Elise is missing, and he wonders if she is still splattered on the side porch.

He ignores the thought and speaks directly to Mr. Shirley.

"I need time to get some things together and then I'll come out."

The old man stares at him for several seconds and then offers an almost imperceptible nod.

"I think he believes you," Chris says.

"I wasn't lying. We are going out there." He also knows that if Chris's plan does not work, he will give himself to save the Millers. "I'm going to get some new clothes."

"For fighting?" Chris asks.

"Yeah, but also because I smell like shit."

"Bring some for us," Sarah says.

"Of course."

He walks upstairs and into his room. Elise's eyes flame out of the night to continue their vigil at his window. He turns away from them and toward the clothes on top of his dresser. He dresses in a fresh white shirt, blue jeans, socks, and a fresh pair of sneakers he was going to use for running during the summer before he planned to stay inside. Sarah is about his size, so he grabs a black shirt and jeans for her. The only clothes he has large enough for Chris are a red shirt and black sweatpants that he thinks are his father's, and they are in his closet. He only hesitates once before ripping away the duct tape and letting the door fold open. He grabs the set from the pile on the closet floor.

He risks one glance back at Elise before leaving the room.

Cloves of garlic and two candles line the front door. Silver chains and forks from his mother's fine china snake across the barrier on the bay windowsill. Seeing his mother's things lying so casually around the house creates a pit in his stomach, but she's the one they need protection against.

He finds his two friends in the master bedroom, sliding the queen-sized bed from the wall. The emergency utility light sits on the floor and illuminates one side of the bedroom so that it can't be seen through the windows. Scott hands the clothes to Sarah and Chris and takes their place as they change, moving the bedside nightstand to the other side of the room.

"I won't look at you in your undies," Chris says with a goofy smile.

"Shit, go for it. One last thrill before we die." She laughs.

Scott wants to be jealous, but the situation it too terrifying not to have a little sense of humor.

"Actually, I saw something in the basement that might be useful." Chris walks out of the room as Sarah takes off her shirt and jeans. Scott busies himself with his mother's dresser. A wooden box falls to the floor and spills gold jewelry across the carpet. He fights the urge to pick up the pieces by concentrating on the task at hand. On the dresser he spots an envelope with his name written with careful, perfect cursive.

Her final gift to you. Before she wanted you dead.

Even if that is true, it doesn't matter. He has lives he has to try to and save.

Lives that are in danger because—

Someone's mother is about to die, Sarah's words echo. That is all that matters at this moment.

Chris returns with a handsaw and cuts through the flowery wallpaper without making too much sound. Plaster and dust puff out and cause Chris to sneeze a few times, which he muffles with his meaty arm. A few minutes later, he finishes carving out a four-by-four-foot hole. He threads his arm between both planks of wood and pushes with his hand and elbow. Wood cracks from within as he spreads the frame apart. He grabs the saw to carve a hole through the plaster on the other side, but stops when the metal teeth screech. He grabs the flashlight from the floor and looks inside.

"There's shelving with a bunch of shit on it," he says. "I'd push it over, but they'll hear it."

"Let me see if I can slide through," Scott says.

Scott leans into the hole and tears chunks out of the plaster until he can see a row of paint cans sitting on the shelf. He pulls them through and hands them to Sarah one by one, then tears away more of the wall until the hole is big enough for him to fit through. He leans in and rests his forearms on the empty shelf. He tests its sturdiness and then pulls himself forward. With his upper body on top of the shelf, he reaches down with both hands to brace his fall as he lets gravity take him onto the concrete floor. He pulls drip pans, brushes, and a toolbox off the shelves so he can pull the whole unit away from the wall without making too much noise. When completed, he helps Chris and Sarah into the room.

So much landscaping equipment has been hoarded inside the garage over the years that the concrete floor is barely visible.

Broken mowers and tangled weed-whackers littered the garage. His father worked on the yard and the pool with such feverish intent that there had been no room for their car to fit inside for as far back as he can remember, and although half of the tools were either dull or out of power, he swore that he would one day fix them, a statement that always started an argument between his parents.

They find various items to use as weapons. Scott pulls apart the metal clasp that holds two shear blades together, each the size of his arm, and sticks them into his waist. Chris tucks a few screwdrivers into the large pockets of his sweatpants and grabs a shovel near the door. The spade is still caked with mud, which Scott reasons is from his father's tomato digging the night before. Sarah finds a nail gun on one of the shelves and holds the point of a six-inch nail up to her eyes.

"We don't know if any of this is even going to hurt them," she says.

"Mr. Shirley recovered quickly from being run down by an ambulance," Scott says, "but it definitely stalled him. Aim for the knees or other soft parts."

"If they try to grab you, go for the elbow or shoulder," Chris says. "Or we can just try to cut their heads off and be done with it."

"We don't know if that will kill them," Sarah says. "Shadow pulled back together after being torn apart." She grabs a battery from a charger and clicks it into the gun. She pulls the trigger to ensure that it's charged and then pockets a bunch of nails for refilling. "Or maybe they can be cured."

"Are you willing to bet our lives on that?" Chris asks.

"Are you willing to bet theirs?" she says.

"I don't know. If this is an infection, and it started with Mr. Shirley, maybe killing him will cure the others?"

"We have no idea what rules this thing plays by," Scott says, "So let's just concentrate on getting the Millers inside."

Scott crawls back through the hole in the master bedroom. He opens the front door and several pairs of eyes attune to his presence.

Move, he begs on wavering legs. Just. Move.

You are going to die.

He steps out of the door and then hops over the porch's railing, landing on the ground under the bay window. He runs to the side of the house as he glares backward to ensure that the horde is following. Bastion barks wildly as he leads Karen and Elizabeth Campbell in the chase. He runs up the side porch and toward the backyard gate where their daughter appears. She leaps forward, be he's ready. He crashes into her, sending her body sideways off the porch. He opens the gate and runs the length of the pool while watching in his peripherals that the others are giving chase.

"Now!" He screams as loud as he is able then hears the garage door opening.

Bastion is nearly on his heels when he gets to the gate on the other side of the house. He jumps up and grabs the top, wincing as the metal spokes cut into his hands. He pushes through the pain and lifts himself up. Bastion bites the cuff of his jeans and tears a section of it away as Scott rolls over the fence and lands on the other side. He runs toward Mr. Shirley, passing the open garage where Chris and Sarah join his pursuit.

Scott pulls out one of the blades and moves toward Mr. Shirley. The old man lifts David higher in the air as Dan wraps both of his hands around his wife's neck. Scott ignores the threats and stabs the old man above the elbow. The boy drops to the ground and falls onto his back.

Chris swings the shovel and cracks it over Dan's head. The man falls and releases his wife. Chris moves to help her up, but Bastion tackles him across the lawn.

"Chris," Sarah yells and rushes toward him. She lifts the nail gun and fires two into Bastion's side. The dog yelps as its body topples, giving Chris enough chance to stand.

"Get them," Chris yells as he picks up the shovel, referring to the boy and his mother.

Sarah helps lift Nancy off the ground and joins Scott with moving her son toward the porch. Mr. Shirley reaches forward with his unwounded arm and grabs Scott's shirt, pulling him into a bear hug tight enough to pin his arms to his side and render the blade in his hand useless.

Chris swings the spade at Mr. Shirley's legs, buckling his knees. Scott gasps for air as Mr. Shirley continues his embrace.

Sarah and Nancy lead the boy toward the porch. Dan appears with his cracked, bloody skull, which does not seem to have impeded his movement. He grabs Nancy and hauls her to the side, tackling and then straddling her body. Sarah's instinct is to let go of David, but the Campbells are already running into view from the side of the house.

"Save David," Nancy screams.

Sarah hesitates, but knows it is the right move.

"Mom," David cries as Sarah struggles to pull the boy onto the porch. She sees Chris already attacking Mr. Shirley's loosening arms and takes that bit of hope to prioritize the boy's safety. She opens the door and pulls the boy inside the house, closing the door behind them but not letting go of the doorknob to be ready to let her friends inside.

Scott falls onto the grass as Mr. Shirley releases him. He swings the blade as he turns around and slices the old man across his face.

"Now, Scott," Chris yells as he lifts the spade above his head. Scott knows that the strike will bisect the old man's head. If Scott helps separate the head and does enough damage to the body, it might take longer to pull itself together, just like Shadow's body.

Elise jumps onto Chris's side and digs her teeth into his biceps. He screams and drops the shovel to grab her.

Scott pushes Mr. Shirley over and shoves the shears into Elise's head. She drops to the grass. The painful knowledge of hurting a little girl is fleeting due to immediately seeing her pulling the shear out of her head.

You just gave her a weapon, you idiot.

"Scott, here," Chris yells while clasping his arm and heading toward the ambulance.

Scott looks back to see the Campbells, Bastion, and Mr. Shirley flanking him on all sides. Dan is on top of Nancy, throwing up discolored viscera into her mouth. Scott's stomach churns, but he can't afford to wait for it to evacuate. He weaves through Elise and Elizabeth and reaches Chris, who is struggling to lift himself up and into the driver's side door. Scott pushes Chris's bottom up as hard as he can, sending his friend yelling as he rolls into the van. He pulls himself up just in time for Bastion and Elizabeth to reach the ambulance. He grabs the driver's side door and closes before they can reach inside.

"I got fucking bit," Chris cries in the passenger seat. "Am I infected?" The genuine worry on his face breaks Scott's heart.

"I just saw Dan shove throw up into his wife's mouth. I'm assuming that's how they get infected."

"Are you sure?" Chris cries.

"No, but other than tremendous amounts of pain, are you having any 'kill Scott' thoughts?"

"Not more than usual," Chris says with a glint of hope in his eyes. This must have renewed his vigor, because he climbs over Scott and into the bed of the ambulance. A gurney and several bottles of antiseptic are lying about, but the cabinets are all locked and under plexiglass in case of an accident. Chris opens a bottle of antiseptic and screams as he pours it over his arm. When the bottle is empty, he fishes keys from one of his pockets and opens a cabinet on the floor. He pulls out a roll of medical bandages and wraps it around his arm. He uses his teeth to rip an end off and then shoves the roll into another deep pocket.

The ambulance starts to teeter as the infected try to push it over.

"Here," Chris says, and throws Scott the ring of keys as he nods toward the ceiling at a four-foot-long metal case. He unlocks it and finds a red axe with a sharp silver tip mounted on the side of the vehicle.

"That helps," he says. He lifts the axe off its mount and hands it to Chris and then pulls the last shear from the side of his jeans. "But we can't get past them all."

"I had an idea about that," Chris says, and points toward the two oval windows in the bay doors. The plexiglass is cracked, but still Scott can see the manhole cover entrance to the drainage sewer.

That was a good time down there, Scotty.

Scott swore he would never go down there again, but it's not the worst idea.

"Yeah," he relents. "Might as well."

They step carefully to the back and ready to open it. Nancy Miller's newly infected face appears in one of the windows.

"We didn't save her," Scott says.

"We saved her son," Chris states, as though it is an acceptable answer.

Scott looks away, and a glint of silver catches his attention. He knows what it is immediately. He hasn't stopped thinking about it since it went missing.

He kneels and picks up his mother's silver necklace with the peridot gem.

"Why do you have this?" Scott asks with utter confusion as he lifts it into the air. "How did you..." he looks up at Chris, who is staring back at him and the necklace with a look akin to fear. The color drains from his face.

"I... I'll explain later. We need to go—"

The driver's side door opens, and Elizabeth jumps inside.

Chris kicks the bottom door open, hitting Nancy and toppling her to the asphalt. He jumps down and runs for the manhole cover.

What the hell did he do? You don't think...

Scott shakes the thought away because he needs to concentrate on running away. He pockets the necklace and jumps out of the ambulance before Elizabeth grabs him.

"We won't make it," he says as he sees the horde round the ambulance.

Chris drops the axe and pulls out two screw drivers from his pocket. He shoves them into the open notch in the manhole cover and strains against its weight.

Scott raises the shears and braces for the wave of infected bodies.

Chris tilts the metal cover away from the opening to crash against the blacktop. "You first!" He yells.

Scott doesn't hesitate to turn his back on the infected, but he hesitates when he stares into the dark hole. He has not been down there in years, when he first heard the voice in his head. He has never wanted to forget anything more in his life until his mother died.

Go on Scotty, let's take a trip down memory sewer.

Scott closes his eyes and jumps inside.

CHAPTER NINE

SCOTT LANDS HARD AND twists his ankle, sending him to the smelly, sticky water flowing through the sewer. He cries out in pain and hears his parents yelling from the circle of light above. He pushes away the pain so he can get to his feet and keep moving before his father can catch him. No amount of pain will compare to what his father will do to him, having been so defiant, so disobedient.

He doesn't see the world like you now see it, full of scary possibilities. He doesn't know the codes or the rituals to keep the bad things away.

He leans against the brick and moves forward. He expected more water, at least up to his knees, and not the tiny stream that is barely high enough to wet his shoes.

Let's hope it doesn't rain.

"What if it does? Scott asks.

"Keep talking," his father's voice echoes. "I'll find you." He sounds more worried than mad.

That's a trick. He's going to hurt you.

He hurries until he reaches a split in the tunnel.

Left, straight, or right?

What feels better?

Left.

Why?

I don't know.

Trust your instincts.

He turns left and the light that he had been using to travel is gone.

"I'm scared," he says.

You probably put the code in wrong.

"I did exactly as you asked."

Are you sure?

Tears fall, followed by sobs and whimpers. His weaker foot scrapes the ground and causes the pain in his ankle to rise into his body. Another sharp pain in his head as he hits a stone wall. He can turn left or right, but both directions seem even darker than this tunnel.

"Scott."

His father's voice is behind him, but when he turns, he can't see anyone. He crumbles to the ground and puts his hands on his head. He cries hysterically, and then screams as he feels something on his back.

"It's okay, Scott, it's Dad."

Scott looks up and sees his father's face.

"I'm sorry," Scott says.

"It's okay," his father assures, rubbing his back and then embracing him with one arm.

"Don't hurt me," Scott begs.

His father hugs him. "We will discuss your punishment later."

"No," Scott screams and beats against his father's arm as he carries him back to the opening. He doesn't want to stay down in the dark, but he also does not want to be hurt.

"You were supposed to protect me," Scott says.

His father stops and looks at him. The older man looks sad, even hurt.

"I'm protecting you from yourself," he says, and then continues down the tunnel.

You were supposed to put in the code right. Stop messing everything up.

"I'm sorry," he says.

"I'm sorry, too," his father replies. "You will never come down here again."

———◆◇◆———

THE TUNNEL IS SMALLER than he remembers, yet still as terrifying.

He turns away from the darkness he will have to run through to make sure Chris is on his way down.

"It's only six feet deep," he yells as Chris as he lowers himself through the hole. He moves out of the way as Chris drops and then stumbles against the slimy brick wall. Scott helps him straighten up just as a shadow cuts the moonlight from above. One of the infected is already jumping down.

"Your turn," Scott yells and pushes Chris ahead.

The light from the outside diminishes with each step, and the narrow space amplifies their pursuers' footfalls as they close in. Scott scrapes a hand along the left wall to keep his balance. Chris stops at an intersection of three tunnels and doesn't hesitate to take the one on the left toward the house. A few feet further down, Scott hears a separate trickle of water and realizes too late that they have reached the house. The air flies out of his lungs as he hits Chris's back.

Chris's exhale echoes as he gets pinned between Scott and the basement wall.

Although he is still catching his breath, Chris holds the axe in both hands and uses the blade's curved backside to punch through the already cracked wall.

While Chris attacks the wall, Scott turns and faces the darkness with his shear at the ready, knowing that the infected will appear inches from his face in a matter of seconds.

A chunk of concrete, wide enough for them to squeeze through, cracks off and topples into the basement.

Chris grabs the back of his shirt and pulls him through the opening. They fall a few feet into the flooding basement as two pairs of infected arms reach through the hole.

"Help me," Chris says as he pulls a full shelf from the corner of the room. Scott stands and slices the arms with his shear, but they are not deterred. He stabs at the hints of faces in the dark, pushing them away from the opening. The infected scream. Scott does not recognize them as screams of pain, but annoyance.

Chris drags the shelf over the entrance, and they pack it with everything they can find. The infected continue to try and break through, but they use separate shelf to brace the other against the wall. They wait until the infected's attacks cease.

Satisfied that it is immovable, they sit on the floor.

Chris wraps an arm around Scott's shoulder. They pant frantically until their breathing regulates. Chris's face is covered in nicks and scratches, but nothing that looks too bad. Blood paints the bandages on his arms, but they will just need redressing. They stare at each other for a moment, and whether it is from exhaustion, fear, or the impossible fact that they are still alive, they laugh.

"The fun just keeps amping up, eh, Scotty?"

"No." Scott waves in the air and shakes his head. "It's not funny," he says, even though he can't stop laughing.

"Of course it isn't. That's why we have to laugh." Chris places his forehead against Scott's. "We saved the kid."

Scott nods. At least stepping outside was not as disastrous as he had feared.

Chris stands, and then yells through the hole in the ceiling, "Sarah, it's us! Don't kill us." Sarah doesn't reply.

"Sarah?" Scott calls. Chris helps him push the table up. He lifts himself into the hallway and moves into the living room.

Sarah is lying on the floor. Her eyes are filled with fear, pleading for help as she holds her hand against her neck to stop her blood from gushing out. It pours across the carpet, glistening under the candlelight.

CHAPTER TEN

GIVE UP, PLEASE.

Scott kneels and takes off his shirt to push against the bite in her neck. Her eyes widen and her mouth opens to a silent scream.

Scott cries, "I'm sorry, I—"

Chris's arm wraps around his chest and pulls him to his feet. "I know you're scared," he says as he squeezes Scott's body in his arms. "I am too. I'll help her while you find the thing that did this to her." He throws Scott behind him and then drops to his knees to inspect Sarah.

"Is she..." Scott cries.

"It won't matter if whatever is inside lets the others in," Chris seethes through his teeth.

"What if she's—"

Chris turns to look up at him. "Still alive?" He picks up the axe and tosses it. Scott catches it and says, "Okay," as the ceiling thumps with something moving across the second floor.

He takes the stairs with the point of the axe pointing ahead. *Chris should be doing this. He's much stronger.*

But he has the knowledge to help Sarah.

You're so fucking useless.

He reaches the landing and looks around the room. Silent, undisturbed.

A ripping noise from his left.

He turns his head in time to see the closet door slowly cascading open.

He pivots his body toward it and moves into the center of the room, holding the axe blade forward, trying to keep it from shaking under his terrified hands.

Scream as it kills you so you can at least alert your friends.

Scott uses the tip of the blade to touch the side of the door and push it open. The darkness within is endless.

Do it, he tells himself. Prove that when it matters, you will not be afraid.

Run away screaming.

He takes a step toward the closet.

Something wraps around his ankles and pulls.

The side of his head hits the floor. He tries to pull free, but whatever has a hold of him is too strong. He fights to flip his body over and then curls to look at his feet. The boy's youthful hands are reaching out from under the bed and pulling him with an adult's strength. Scott lifts the axe, aims between his legs, and thrusts it forward. The boy releases a sound that is a mix of a scream and a growl. The blade gives a slight resistance as he tugs the axe back. He aims to strike again, but one of the hands lets go of his ankle and grabs the blade. It yanks it from Scott's hands and pulls it under the bed. The hand returns and grabs at his jeans, but instead of pulling him under, the boy pulls himself out, climbing up Scott's body until they are face-to-face.

The boy opens his mouth and releases a glob of purple ooze. Scott covers his face and feels the viscera splash across his forearms. He balls his fists and punches David's face, then leans his body to the side to buck the boy off. Scott rolls over and straddles the boy's chest. He wraps one hand around his neck while his other reaches for a hardback from the bookshelf.

"Mr. Scott," David cries. The disease is gone and only the ten-year-old's frightened face remains. "Mr. Scott, please stop hurting me."

Scott drops the book and crawls backwards until his back hits the opposite wall.

"No," he says, regretting his retreat, "I'm not falling for this." He balls his fists and stands.

David sits up and hugs his legs to cry into his knees. "I want my mom. He hurt my mom."

He does not know if David is really talking, but one word catches his attention. "He?"

"He's whispering in my head. It hurts," he sobs.

"Are you sure it's a 'He'? Not a 'She'?"

David shakes his head. "He is stealing my thoughts and moving me around. He wants to talk to you."

"What's he saying, David?"

The boy's sobbing turns into a scream and his hands squeeze his head. "Stop!"

"David, it's okay." The boy's pain is difficult to witness. "Tell me what he's saying."

David tries to catch his breath while still crying, the staccato of sobs that only a suffering child can make. "He wants to be inside."

"Inside? The house?"

"I don't know," David says, shaking his head.

"Is he listening?"

David furrows his brow and looks at his knees. "I think so."

"What do you want?" Scott asks.

David screams.

"David, what's wrong? What's he doing?"

"He's making my head hurt again," he cries. His eyes close tightly. Then, his eyes open wide as he says, "Mom."

Scott's body chills, and the room starts to spin. He leans against the wall to keep himself upright. "What about that? Why did he say that?" The words leave him angrily and cause the boy to cry harder. "I'm sorry, David. I'm not mad at you. Is there anything else it's saying?"

"He's stealing my words."

Stealing his words, Scott thinks. It's not just speaking through him, it's reading his mind. Learning from it.

"He wants you to go outside so he can get inside."

"He wants to come inside the house? If I let him, will he let us leave?"

David shakes his head more violently. His throat gargles and pockets of the purplish abrasions bubble across his face.

"You," David forces out of a clogged-sounding throat. "Inside you."

The boy bounds forward onto his feet and then tackles Scott against the wall. Scott tries to push him away, but the boy has stopped attacking. His body is still and his eyes are glazed over.

Somehow, Scott knows David is no longer in control.

"Who are you?"

The boy's head tilts.

"I am nothing."

Scott tries to find the best questions to ask. If this thing is trying to pluck out words and thoughts from its victims, he can assume that it is still learning, still trying to communicate and navigate within the world.

"Where do you come from?"

"Nothing," it answers without hesitation. "Empty." It winces, and David's real voice whimpers through, intertwining with the sound of the disease in the back of his throat. "Dark. I come from dark."

"How did you get out of the dark?"

David's head shakes. "There was nothing, then there was everything."

"How do you know about me?" Scott asks the question without thinking about it, or regardless of the consequence of knowing that the answer might have something to do with his mother.

"I learned it from him."

"Him?" Did that mean his father did this?

Chris's voice tunnels up from the bottom of the stairwell. "Scotty, are you okay?"

The disease bursts from David's face as he reaches for Scott.

Scott shoves a shoulder into the boy's chest and sends him across the room. The disease bursts through the boy's arms, tendrils wrapping around David's hands and extending away from each finger until they look like enormous claws. It swings through the air but is interrupted by Chris grabbing its wrist and turning it around until it breaks. The boy screams a mixture of human and inhuman. Chris shoves it toward the bed and it collapses onto it.

"Front door," Chris says. He ties David's talons around his back and pulls up his body. The boy thrashes against Chris's grip.

Scott takes the stairs first, unlocks the deadbolt, and throws open the door.

The infected are there, but unmoving, as in a trance.

"Ready?" Chris says, struggling against the screeching infected boy on the living room landing. Scott remembers that the thing was trying hard to search the boy's mind, and must have had to let go of the others to have the energy to do so.

Scott steps aside to let Chris shove the boy out of the doorway. David's body falls down the porch and rolls across the grass. The other infected awaken, and again, they stare at Scott in unison. He slams the door and locks the deadbolt. He turns around to see that Sarah is no longer in the living room, only the terrifyingly large stain from her blood is present.

"Chris," Scott's throat cracks. "Is Sarah..."

"I moved her into the bedroom."

He lets out a sigh of relief. At least he has Chris to look out for them.

I learned it from him.

Scott forms a terrible thought, but one that makes as little and as much sense as any other he has had when confronted with this horror. He had assumed his father had dug up the body, either accidentally releasing the disease or intentionally. But there is another possibility that has been in front of him all night. An idea that has haunted him since seeing his two closest friends back together.

Scott fishes his mother's pendant and holds it in the air. The pendant twists on its chain. A smack of dark brown, almost red, stains the back side of the peridot.

"My mother loved you," he says.

"I know," Chris says, looking at the pendant. Seeing it drains the color from his face again.

He did this for Sarah.

Sarah said Chris had a secret, and they obviously were together in some way when Scott was locked inside. Was this Chris's way of getting what he wanted? Had witnessing those deaths during medical training numbed him so much that he would do this? Chris knew about infectious diseases. Knew exactly what this one was.

His father didn't do this for his mother.

Chris did this for Sarah.

Chris was the bad man all along.

"Why did you do it?"

Chris furrows his brow. He opens his mouth, but then shuts it.

"How did you know?" He asks.

Scott's anger explodes through the numbness. He lifts a leg and kicks Chris in the stomach, bending him over. He opens the door and waits for Chris to stand.

"What are you doing?"

"You made this happen," Scott says. "You fix it."

He kicks Chris in the chest, sending him out of the doorway and falling down the steps. He closes the door as the infected rush toward his best friend.

Chris's scream abruptly stops.

Scott does not know if Chris can fix what he had started, but regardless, another family member had been taken by his hand.
Scott lost his brother.

CHAPTER ELEVEN

SARAH IS WRAPPED IN the comforter on the master bed and staring at the ceiling. Scott checks her pulse and finds it weak.

"I'm infected," she says to no one in particular.

"We don't know that." He sits at the edge of the bed near her knees and places a hand on her thigh above the covers.

"That thing spit shit into my neck, Scott. I can feel it crawling inside me. It's violating me."

"I need to put an end to this," he says, pulling a strand of black hair off her hazel eyes and tucking it behind her ear.

"Where's Chris?" she asks.

Yeah, Scott. Tell her what you did.

"I talked to it," he says. "The disease, or whatever is controlling it."

"What is it?" Sarah tries to sit up but winces and then falls back to the bed.

"I still don't really know, but it said that he learned about me and that's why it wants to infect me."

Sarah stares at the ceiling, her face contorting with the information. "It's not just spreading on instinct and focusing on you. It has a mind of its own and can make decisions. Could it really be your mother?"

"It says it learned if from a man." Tears release, but he doesn't bother wiping them away. No strength for himself remains.

Sarah is contemplative for a moment, then she asks again with a crack in her voice, "Scott, where's Chris?"

Scott stands from the bed. "I'm done, Sarah. I tried to share your reasoning, your optimism, but I won't let it take you. I'm going out there." He leans over so that his face hovers above hers. He stares into her hazel eyes and the kisses her. She returns the kiss, chastised at first, but then adds pressure. The kiss lingers. Tears from each other's eyes spread salt across their lips.

"Don't leave me, Scott," she cries. Then, she whispers, "Don't give your life for mine."

Scott turns to leave the room. He wants to tell her something like "I love you" or "Remember me," but the purpose of his life is as unknowable as the events of that night. The happiness, the suffering. Lives cut short. What was the whole point of any of it?

He walks away, but stops when he sees the card from his mother on top of the dresser.

"Here," he says, picking up the envelope and laying it at her side. "This is the last thing my mother left me. I feel like you should have it."

He opens the front door and walks onto the porch. As before, the infected corral and move across the lawn and then stop in unison. Chris is in the middle of them, skin infected, eyes no longer aware of their history.

Mr. Shirley continues his stance in the center of the infected. Scott wonders the merit of trying to destroy the old man to see if the others become untethered. Might be worth trying as a final effort if taking him out will release the others.

"Is there a way we can end this with my friends getting out alive?"

The infected across the lawn shudder in unison. Then, Mr. Shirley speaks. As with David, only a hint of his natural voice is heard underneath a throat coated with disease.

"Inside you. No one else."

"How can I know that's true?"

"Don't need others for life."

Chris drops to the ground. The sludge and viscera melt from his body like ice cream on hot concrete. His eyes are closed, but he is breathing.

Scott's breath catches and he nearly faints from the sight and the slice of hope for… everyone.

"Scott," Chris pleads, looking up at him with eyes full of history. "He's telling the truth."

"Okay," he says. "I'm going to go say goodbye, and then let you in."

He deadbolts the door out of habit.

As he turns around, Sarah is leaning on the opposite wall, barely able to keep herself upright. She is pale, her eyes are bloodshot. She is in her final moments and looks as though she is about to collapse. Scott moves to her in case she does.

A piece of paper falls from her hand.

"Read," she croaks, and then places a hand on the wall to brace herself as she moves through the living room towards the front door.

Scott tries to follow her, but she lifts her other hand.

"Read the card," she whispers, energy continuing to drain. "It's important."

He picks up the card. A black cat holds a balloon on the front, its face stained with Sarah's blood. The inside is full of his mother's perfect cursive, written with blue ink.

Sarah unlocks the door.

"What the hell are you doing?" Scott's heart races.

Sarah turns around and calmly stares at him.

"No," he says, looking into her eyes that now gleam with a purple hue. Small patches of red seep from the pours of her face.

A piece of himself breaks and he knows that this is the moment he has chosen to give up. He will take the deal and be over with it all. Die to save his friends.

There are worse deaths.

"Listen to me, Scott," she forces the words out like something is holding them back. "Read what she wrote and then come save us all." She opens the door and despite seeing the infected standing at the bottom of the porch, she doesn't hesitate to step outside.

Scott screams and reaches for her, but she shuts the door before he can grab her.

Scott collapses.

Everything he has ever loved is gone.

Every nightmare he has ever had has come alive.

Just as I told you it would.

"You told me you would protect me," he cries. All you've ever done is make me afraid.

And now all those fears have come to light.

Scott balls his fists, bending the card.

Read it. Maybe it will tell you why the woman you love would rather die than be with you.

He wants to protest, but even now he can't help but place his trust and love in Sarah. With nothing left, he honors her final wish and reads the words in the card.

The first time he reads it, he cries hysterically, his mind racing at the words and their implications. The second time, he processes the information being revealed. The third time, he cries - and laughs - with abandon, understanding why Sarah felt it was so important for him to read the letter.

He drops to his knees and screams, not from fear or anguish, but also not from joy or happiness. He cries from the revelation that has been laid before him. The letter is only one page long, front and back, but the words add new context to his entire life.

This letter has changed his past, present, and - with any luck - his future.

He laughs and cries, and his words fill the empty house.
"I have a brother."

INTRUSION II

RENOVATION

DEAR SON,

You're a man now, which means that the ties that bind us together have to come undone whether I want them to or knot. (See what I did there?) We both know that's never going to happen. You will always be my baby and I will always do what I can to keep you safe. I'm not letting go. I am, however, going to tell you the truth. I have been hard on you, and I know that my careful love has caused you anguish.

Even though a mother ALWAYS knows best, I have many regrets, and some of them have affected you. I'm not telling you this to excuse my actions, but to explain them in a way that you might understand when you become a parent.

You were not alone when you were born. You had a brother, but he was afflicted with a rare skin condition that killed him seconds after birth. Some say it was a blessing, because he would have had a sheltered life, with a bad immune system, sensitive skin, and possibly brain damage. He was able to accomplish one thing in his short time; he kept you alive. The doctors said it was a miracle that you survived unaffiliated, but I believe it was your brother keeping you safe. That's a fantasy I hold on to and one that I try to remind myself of every time I hold you back from living. Unfortunately, my fear of losing another child gets the best of me.

I tried to have him buried in the family plot at Samuel's Church, but since he was unbaptized, Father Daniels (our former family priest) was unwilling to do it without performing the ritual on both of you at the same time. Your Dad was furious and threatened to bury your brother in the cemetery without the church's consent. We protested to the diocese but had not heard back for such a long time that we decided to bless your brother with our own ritual.

We buried him in the backyard, and for the past few months I have been growing the tomatoes in his honor, and to harvest them for dinner for both of your eighteenth birthdays. I'm sorry I never told you, but between the betrayal I felt from the church, the questions about my faith that it caused, and the loss of a child, I needed to push it all away and concentrate on you. Sometimes that concentration comes out as strict and controlling.

I have started seeing a therapist and will be working on alleviating some of the trauma and anxiety. I have a condition called obsessive-compulsive disorder. Symptoms include extreme anxiety, depression, loss of control that makes me repeat actions, and intrusive thoughts (basically—the negative, terrified voice in my head is literally a voice in my head). I have taken this condition out on you and have seen signs that you might have it as well.

My birthday present to you is this: I will do my best to fight the monsters in my head, and to ensure that if you have the same monsters, you do not have to fight them alone.

Some people grow up to be like their parents, some grow up despite them. I'm not going to claim that I ever know what I am doing, only that I try my best to pro—I was just about to write "protect," but that's the wrong word - I try my best to keep you happy. In the end, it's all about maintaining that beautiful smile on your face.

You have grown into a man that is kinder and stronger than I could have ever imagined. My hope is that even with my failings, you can take the better parts of my love and forgive the rest. Please remember, just because you are grown doesn't mean your mother isn't there to protect you. I will look out for you until the day I die, and if there is a God, and he is willing, even after.
Happy 18th Birthday.
Love, Mom.

Chapter Twelve

Scott folds the letter before his tears can drop onto the paper and smear the ink. He assembles memories like puzzle pieces to try and find the whole picture. The two cribs in the basement. His father turning the upstairs into one room when his parents decided not to try for another child. His mother's overbalance and his father's detachment.

The infected neighbors, their aggression, and moving as if by one person. The timing of it happening on his birthday and their focus on him. A twin brother who died of a disease that connected to his mind and retained his psyche, the mind of newborn. It had been festering in the ground for eighteen years until its body was uprooted—

Uprooted.

Scott runs into the back room and opens the door to snatch a tomato from the garden where his brother's remains have been exhumed. He digs his thumbs in and pulls it apart. The inside is oozing a thick substance with a purple hue. The plants grew through the body and the disease latched on. His father delivered these to Mr. Shirley that morning. The old man must have eaten one and became another host for the disease.

Everyone wants you dead.

Scott looks at the letter and remembers the words. "I don't believe that," he says. For the first time since leaving the house that night so many months ago, he is convinced that neither his mother nor father blame him for what happened.

Then why did he dig up the corpse? Why did he tell your brother to get a redo inside of you?

"Will you shut the hell up?" He yells.

Why? Because you don't want to hear the truth?

"Because it's not true. Nothing you say is true. You have done nothing but hold me back."

I've protected you more than your own mother has. I've even protected you from your mother.

"All you have done is made me afraid of things that haven't happened, and were probably not going to happen. I created you to protect me from everything I'm afraid of, because I feel like I don't have control."

This is all about me, he thinks. My mother died, and I'm in a tremendous amount of grief and an incredible amount of guilt from feeling like it was my fault. I shut myself inside because I was too afraid to interact with the world where such un-meaningful things and terrible suffering can happen. But her death only exacerbated something that was already there. I was always this terrified. I seconded guessed every step out of my mother's womb to the point my anxiety created endless scenarios of death, suffering, and sadness to trick my conscience mind into jumping through hoops in order to placate its fear. Hell, I even created an annoying voice to hound me.

To haunt you.

I inherited the same mental illness that my mother suffered from, and despite every way my mind tried to fight it, I still ended up with my friends suffering from a sentient disease that has the mind of my twin brother that I didn't know I had because the world actually is all suffering.

No, not all. Not if I have to try to take control. Not if I have the power to do something about it. He stares down at the tomato in his hands and the ichor within.

Are you about to do something crazy?

'Someone's mother is about to die,' Sarah had said that night. 'Do something.'

He closes his eyes and raises the tomato to his mouth.

What if nothing happens?

Then there is nothing to be afraid of.

Despite the infection, or maybe because of it, the first taste is deliciously sweet.

And with the first swallow, he is no longer looking through his own eyes...

He sees with many eyes. They stare at the front of his house from different angles like spider's eyes. Thoughts come along with those eyes, filling his head with memories and ideas that are not his experiences, minds that are not his own. A middle-aged woman, a young boy, an old man.

The entity that ties their minds together is strongest in the old man's. Its strength diminishes with every copy of itself, stretching out from Mr. Shirley's mind to the others.

He tries to block out the entity and concentrate only on Mr. Shirley. The more he does, the more he knows the old man's thoughts.

He sees through Mr. Shirley's eyes. A tomato is in Mr. Shirley's hand. He takes a bite and thinks about the woman who grew them, how he misses her and hopes her family is okay. Her son has not left the house since it happens, and his heart breaks for the boy. His heart also breaks for the boy's father, who lost a wife who had lost a son in childbirth. A twin, in fact, and although he is grateful that one survived, it must be unnerving to know that had the baby survived, it would have looked exactly like their other child. It must be haunting.

Scott pushes the thoughts away.

The old man's body is the progenitor of the infections outside, but still is not the source. The source is in a distant place where it can't leave but continues to grow. It yearns to move, to find a place to rest. It thinks it knows where to go and how to get there.

Get inside. Inside. How. Inside. Someone who is more connected to the inside. The boy. Chris. Brother. Love. Sarah. Sarah.

The thoughts disconnect. Each vision goes dark until there is only one.

"Come out, Scott." Sarah's voice calls to him. "Come out and play."

Scott screams awake, his body shakes from fear and his lungs struggle to catch his breath. He fights through it and stumbles down the hallway and into the living room. Through the barrier in the bay windows, he sees Sarah, diseased and motionless.

Scott senses her presence as though she is standing next to him. He knows her thoughts, feels her emotions, and if he focuses, can see through her eyes, or at least what her mind interprets as seeing. In turn, she can sense him too, or rather, the thing that has occupied her mind. It turns her head to look at him through the window and uses her voice to speak aloud.

"I love you, Scott. Come out and play with me."

A piece of his heart pangs from seeing her so violated. The infection growing inside of himself is enabling him to feel her mind - all the infected minds - but not enough to take over his own. The word "immune" occurs to Scott, and with it another connection is made.

His mother wrote that she imagined his brother taking the disease away from him to spare his life. But that is not what happened.

Scott is immune.

All he needs to do is figure out how to break the connection Mr. Shirley has with the others. He's the source of the infection, the inheritor of his brother's mind. If he destroys Mr. Shirley's body, that could sever the connection to the others. Without the other minds, he might be able to sense its source, his brother's remains. But how is he going to fight something that can read his thoughts?

Let them.

Let them? He questions. Sometimes I don't even want to be here—

Scott laughs at his self deprecation. For the first time, his twisted perception can help.

He runs into the kitchen and fishes a glass jar out of the barrier to the side of the house. From his peripheral's, he sees the box that holds the white jacket with the fuzzy brown collar his father gifted. Next to it, wedged between a coffee maker and the bottom of a chair, is the box for the leather watch with a clear face and bronze gears from Sarah. He slips both on and then grabs a flashlight from the floor. The one that Chris says is big and heavy enough to protect him from the dark. He pockets it and then takes the jar off the counter on his way to the living room.

"Okay." He breathes deeply to steady his body and mind. Then he opens the front door. "Come inside."

The infected run towards the house. Mr. Shirley, or as he now understands, an imprint of his brother's psyche using the old man like a marionette, stays behind and waits anxiously. It never felt this emotion, anxiety, but that is a feeling that Scott has had in spades and is willing to share. If this thing wants to be inside his mind, let it have the whole experience.

Scott throws the jar onto the porch. The glass shatters and hundreds of coffee beans rain down the steps, filling the clear summer night with the sound of rain.

Pick every one up, his intrusive voice demands. *Make it right. Gain back control.*

He allows the thoughts to linger and then opens his mind to give them away.

Every infected person stops abruptly at the bottom of the steps, then bends over to pick up the beans. Bastion uses his nose to push them into a pile. Despite the dog's torn, bloody body, it's canine actions are still adorable.

"Yeah," Scott tells the thing inside the old man. "I'm complicated."

Mr. Shirley runs forward, but Scott knows he's not in danger. The old man reaches over the other infected to pluck coffee beans from the grass, one by one.

"Fight it like I've tried to all these years. I'm the one you want. Come inside and play with me." He backs up to the center of the living room and watches as the old man's body walks over the steps, onto the porch, and into the room.

He can feel the disease in the old man's body communicating with his own. Biological transmitters of thought and essence. More than natural or supernatural, he still didn't know. What matters is that he knows what the other is thinking. The thing inside is the old man is rooting through Scott's thoughts to see if he set a trap, or is holding something in his hands.

Scott lifts his empty hands into the air to alleviate its anxiety.

The old man's hand swings down to grab him.

Scott closes the distance and grabs the old man's temple between his hands. The disease around the sores retracts from where his fingers touch. The old man drops to his knees, bringing them eye to eye. Viscera seeps from the old man's pores in a trypophobian nightmare, then flows upwards and around Scott's fingers. He rips the infection away until all that was in Mr. Shirley is now settled around his hands like black gloves. He rips it away from Mr. Shirley's body with enough force to send it sludging across the carpet and along the walls.

Scott feels something familiar. Pain? No. Loneliness? Closer. The kind of pain you feel when you have something and then you don't. A forgotten friend. A severed phone connection. A broken toy.

A loved one, lost.

Mr. Shirley's body collapses.

Scott kneels and cradles the old man's head and checks his neck for a pulse. It is there, but faint. Mr. Shirley opens his eyes.

"Thank you," his raspy voice croaks as he pants for air. "Thank..."

The old man's eyes glaze over, and then his body stills.

Scott cries as he checks Mr. Shirley's pulse again, but doesn't find one. He then searches his mind for the connection to the old man's, but that is also gone.

"I'm sorry, Sir," Scott says. He closes the man's eyes and then lays his head gently on the carpet.

Scott grabs the fireman's axe off the floor and then walks to the open door. His neighbors are backing up on the lawn, the thing controlling them troubled more by what Scott was able to do, than the feelings of anxiety that causes obsessive cleaning that they were gifted.

Yes, Scott pushes his thoughts through the bodies in front of him and toward the source he is beginning to feel in the distance, outside of his street. *I will rip you out of every one of them if I have to.*

He sees the thing's hesitation in the eyes of those surrounding him. Scott feels its next move before he consciously understands it.

"No," he screams and gives chase as the bodies run down the street. The thing controlling them does not need to worry about their physical pain, so they move with inhuman speed.

It's okay, he thinks as he stops in the middle of the street. I know where you're going.

He sensed it when he connected to the disease. Distant, but not too distant. He knows why his father dug up the remains. He knows where he took his brother's body.

Scott fishes Chris's keys from his EMT pants on the floor of the master bedroom. He drives the ambulance off his street and away from his home without worrying about what will happen, or even what *might* happen.

He's going to save Sarah.

He's going to save them all.

After that, he's going to save his brother.

Chapter Thirteen

The church spire is silhouetted against the night sky. It peaks above the trees and low-rise buildings, growing more prominent with each turn. Scott rounds the corner of the street where it is located in town square. The closer he gets the stronger he feels his brother's presence, pulsating like a heartbeat, unseen but pounding in his chest.

His neighbors are waiting for him across the marble steps. Nancy, Dan, and David Miller. Karen, Elizabeth, and Elise Campbell. Bastion.

Sarah and Chris are absent. He can feel them inside the church as well. They are still infected. Waiting.

"Okay," he says. "Do something."

A deluge of rain falls on top of the windowsill. He laughs, remembering the "at least it's not raining" joke. A crack of thunder illuminates the spire and shines off the stained glass like eyes come to life.

Dracula's Castle, indeed.

But how many books has he read about heroes fighting vampires? How many castles has he storm in video games? How many of his own fantasies did he have where he conquered death? He would be lying if he thought that he did not have any fear. He was terrified. Although his knowledge and connection gave him the upper hand, he was still one person against something that could create an army, and whatever it had in store for him inside... he knows there is a greater chance that he will never make it out.

He steps on the gas.

Dracula's Castle, be damned.

The ambulance speeds across the grass. The infected jump from the stairs and rush forward. They fling their bodies against the van while Elizabeth jumps onto the hood. She falls through the windshield, cracking the glass and forcing Scott to shield his face. The front wheels hit the bottom steps and lift into the air. The ambulance turns sideways as it flies upward and then collides into one of the oak doors.

Scott catches himself before falling out of the driver's side window. Elizabeth is turning herself over in the cab, snarling and screaming with abandon as she tries to stand. He grabs the axe from underneath the seat and then uses the sides of the window frame to lower himself onto the step below.

The infected are scattered across the lawn in various forms of damage. Dan is missing half a face and Karen's legs are bent away from her body like clock hands. He does not see Nancy, and wonders if she has been pinned under the ambulance. The kids are covered in blood, but standing, and Bastion is trying to stand as its legs stitch back together. Scott moves away from beneath the ambulance and is drenched by the rain. He looks up and sees that the van is angled up to the top of the door and bowing it inward.

The space looks too small to fit through, but the van is angled high enough for him to reach the stained glass in the recess above it. He doesn't hesitate to jump up and grab the top edge of the van to pull himself onto its side, now its roof. The infected that are able to move run toward him.

The rain cascades down the surface and he slips to his feet, so he swings the pick end of the axe down into the side and uses it to haul himself up. David and Elise slam against the van before trying to climb onto it and the vibration, along with the rain, shakes his feet from under him. He managed to hold on to the axe to keep from falling, and then finds his footing again. Luckily, the kids are not tall enough to jump for the edge to lift themselves up, but they rock the van instead. Before the movement gets too hard to battle, he pulls the axe out and then uses it to reach toward the passenger's window. He hooks the edge with the pick and pulls his body forward.

Elizabeth's diseased hang grabs the side and lifts her head out of the window. He buries his face between his arms in time for the nails on her other hand to graze the top of his head. Pain erupts from where his flesh opens in his scalp. He releases one hand from the axe and grabs the flashlight out of his pocket, swings in an arc and bringing it down on the top of her hand. It cracks and releases its grip, dropping her through the bed and out of the other window to crunch onto the step.

Scott climbs until he is at the front of the ambulance where he can reach for the window's recess. Dan and Karen are haphazardly climbing up the back while still regrowing their missing parts. Dan's hand slips and falls back to the steps and tumbles off, making Scott grateful for the rain.

He throws the axe into the recess and then lifts himself up. Despite the exertion, his body feels strong. A tickle on head forces him to reach up to his wound. He feels it pulling back together unit it disappears. Scott smiles. Dracula, eat your heart out.

He peruses the stained glass and sees that the different colors are sectional. He uses the axe to shatter a hole in a section at the bottom and is careful to push the glass inside to lower the risk of getting cut. He inches through the opening and closer to the inside edge. The cavernous room is dark save for the moonlight coming through the dome in the center. It illuminates the altar and a body that lies across the table.

Chris.

The floor is at least twenty feet below, so he uses the axe pick to lower himself down as much as possible and then pulls it away, dropping the remaining ten feet. His shoes slip on the floor and he lands on his back hard enough to send pain through his entire body. Despite being able to heal, the pain is still debilitating. He has to wait until his body can respond before standing up. He walks forward to the baptismal font to catch himself as his body gains back control.

The crucifix hanging above the altar greets him from the back of the room. He looks away out of fear, but then remembers what happened in his nightmare when he looked away. He lifts his head and forces his eyes to refocus. The crucifix and the statue remain unchanged.

Something else has appeared at the altar.

Although only a silhouette against the moonlight, the bald head and stocky build reveals him as Father Daniel, the priest that presided over his mother's funeral. Scott looks around the large interior, remembering that Father Daniel and a few of the nuns reside in the annex of the church. If the priest was infected, the nuns are most likely skulking around the shadows and waiting for him as well.

The priest unleashes a guttural noise that draws back Scott's attention. The robed man holds himself and shakes as though he is about to explode.

From outside, the other infected scream, a sound so distraught Scott is compelled to turn toward the door. Black, purple-tinted muck oozes from the bowed-in door and drops, parts of itself splattering across the floor and pews. It grows in mass until there is no more to drip down from the door and then slides toward Scott.

He retreats back into his mind and uses his own disease to connect to it. Its surface ripples like water and then it stops moving.

The priest's groans become deafening. Scott turns in time to see him reach out toward Chris. He thinks the man is about to hurt his friend, but the disease rises from Chris's wounds and gathers around the priest's hands. He is absorbing the disease the same way Scott had done to Mr. Shirley. His connection to it weakens and continues up the aisle. He moves out of the way and lifts the axe, but then it passes by him and toward the priest and slips underneath the man's robes.

The priest screams, and he raises his hands to the air. The disease bursts out of his back in two directions and solidifies in the air, creating two giant wings. Scott can only assume that the disease e interpreted something inside of the priest's mind. Something powerful, something that fights and has won battles. A dark angel.

The creature's wings flap. It flies off the chancel and closes the distance between them, with only a second for Scott to react. He dives into a pew as the creature lands on the spot where he had been standing. The marble floor cracks under the talons that have been made from the disease wrapping around his feet. It jumps up and lands a foot on the tops of the pews that Scott lies between. The disease moulds over the man's hands to form claws. Scott lifts the axe's handle in time to shield himself, but the claw slices it apart. He throws the handle at the creature's face and uses the twitch it creates to thrust the blade outward and embed it into the thing's head. With a screech, the priest falls onto the seat.

Scott uses the seat to pull himself up. The rows are lengthy, and the creature is already recovering, so Scott jumps over the back of the pew, then over next, heading toward the altar. The creature's wings flap and take it into the air.

Scott reaches Chris and shakes his body. "I could really use your help," he says.

He turns in time to see the creature pump its wings, fly over the pews, and land in the crossing. Scott musters up the bravery to attack offensively instead of defensively. He pulls out the flashlight, yells, and jumps off the altar, tackling the creature. They roll a few feet down the aisle until the creature grabs Scott in its talons and pins his arms at his side and his body to the floor. He tried to buck the thing off his body, but it is too strong. Although the creature is silhouetted by the light from above, he can tell that it is opening its mouth. Scott realizes that even though he is immune to the infection, if the disease is strong enough to withstand his influence it could rip his body apart from the instead.

Instead of releasing the disease from its mouth, the creature releases a scream. A gold metal post burst from its chest.

Chris stands behind it holding the end of one of the tall candle stands that lines the altar. He tilts the end sideways to push the creature off Scott's body. It slides off the pole and falls next to him, the mucky disease dripping off of him in giant globs and bubbling up from the hole in its chest.

Scott rolls over and digs his hand into the hole. He closes his eyes and feels the consciences of the disease scramble to keep itself inside the body. Scott connects his mind to it and pushes away its influence. The diseases thins, and drips to the floor. Scott pulls his hand out and places it over the wound to close it. The priest, bloody but disease free, collapses.

"Death one, Chris one," Chris says, staring down at the priest.

Scott has never felt so elated to see his best friend. "Want to go for a tiebreaker?" he asks.

Chris smiles and reaches a hand out to help him up.

Scott grabs his friend's hand and is pulled into a breathtaking embrace. Scott returns the hug and allows a moment to enjoy it.

"Sarah's here, somewhere," Scott says.

"Let's go get her," He says. He unscrews the three-pronged candle hold from the other end and rests lifts the pole to rest it on his shoulder.

Scott feels more empowered now that Chris is with him, but the last time they saw each other was when Scott blamed him for these horrors, kicked him in the chest, and left him to fend for himself. "Chris, I'm so sorry that—"

"Don't worry about. I felt all the things you felt. I guess we have the disease to thank for that. You knew I was keeping something from you. It's my fault."

"Was it you and Sarah?" Scott asks, knowing the answer. "Are you together?"

Chris's laugh echoes throughout the church. "God, no, Scotty. I'm not her type."

"Oh," Scott's face turns red. Then what..." he trails off.

"I have to tell you, in case we don't make it through this."

"Okay," Scott says, not knowing what is about to come.

"I killed your mother."

Scott's body turns cold. He does not have the faculties to fully comprehend what Chris had said before he continues to speak. "What did you just say?"

"I was training the night we got the call. I didn't know it was her when we arrived. Hell, I even joked about the world being a safer place without another terrible driver."

He half laughs, half sobs, rubbing his hands on his face and leaving them on his forehead, eyes hidden from Scott's.

"The senior officer attended to one driver and told me to check on the other. The body was face down, but I could tell it was a woman, and when I tried to check her pulse, she rolled onto her back. We immediately recognized each other."

Chris lets out a growl as he lowers his hands and turns his eyes toward the ceiling.

Scott does not dare move for fear of losing his balance and his sanity.

"I looked away from her toward the car to see if you were in there. The thought of losing you and that scared me more than having your mother lying in front of me. I let my training take over and I assessed her damage. She had a few cracked ribs and a deep laceration in her stomach. She was losing a lot of blood, so I tried to keep her awake by telling her that I was there for her and that I would save her because she was my mother, too, and that's what sons do. I panicked. I couldn't think straight, and

I couldn't stop crying. It's not what they train you to do. You need to set your personality aside and save the life in front of you. That's how you get the job done. I was just too scared. Too scared of losing her, and of losing you."

Chris breathes deeply and wipes his tears with trembling hands.

"She smiled at me. Even though she must have seen the look on my face, she smiled. Then her eyes just..."

Chris breathes deeply again and looks at Scott. "When you thought it was her that was coming for you, I was scared because I thought she was coming for me. I should have said something, should have offered to give myself up, but I was willing to risk killing all of us just so you didn't have to find out that I failed you."

Scott turns his back on Chris and sits in the front pew. He has avoided thinking about the moment of her death because he thought the horror would break him. He remembers what she said about her portrait in the hallway, how she was feeling when it was taken and her fear of dying alone, and the fact that her worst fear came true because of him shattered his heart and mind. Now, he is imagining the scene, not as a dark fantasy, but the truth of what happened in her final moment. He stands and walks toward Chris, who looks away and steels his jaw as though he is about to be punched. Instead, Scott places his hands on his friend's shoulders until he returns his attention.

"My mother's biggest fear was dying alone," Scotts says, not holding back the intense emotion he feels. "I have lived every moment since her death knowing that her greatest fear had come true. It has been eating away at me. Now you tell me you were with her, that not only was she not alone when she died, but that the person who was with her was someone she considered to be her son. My brother. My best friend. You didn't kill my mother. You stopped her worst fear from coming true."

Scott places a hand on the back of Chris' neck and pulls their foreheads together.

After a long, silent moment, Chris says, "Can I ask you something?"

Scott lets go and wipes away his tears. "Of course."

"You know I can't figure out basic algebra, but you thought I had enough know-how to unleash a free-thinking disease to do my bidding?"

Scott laughs. Hard. The joyous sound echoes across the room until his body is too exhausted to continue. The door that leads to the corridor that connects the annex bursts open. Two older women in night gowns run into the room, their faces riddled with disease.

"What do we do?" Chris asks as he readies his weapon.

"Find Sarah and then look for a tiny skeleton."

"What?"

"I'll explain later." The infected are close. Scott runs forward and then tackles one over a pew. Chris follows and uses the pole to bat the other against the wall.

They make it to the door, lock it behind them, and then start running down the lightless corridor.

"The disease originated in my twin brother that died in childbirth. My parents buried the body in the backyard and yesterday my father dug up the remains and brought them here to force the church to bury them with my mother. The disease attached to the tomatoes my mother planted before she died and Mr. Shirley ate one. That's why he was first to be infected and how the disease knew about my connection to its original host. My brother."

"So it wasn't your mother at all?" Chris asks as the corridor opens to a small round room with a desk and two doors. Along the walls are paintings of the Virgin Mary with her child. Cradling him in her arms. Lifting him up to the sun surrounded by amazed onlookers. Animals surrounding them as they lie in a manger.

The echo of the creatures breaking through the door catches up with them. They move across the room and stop as one of the other two doors open and a figure steps inside.

"No," Scott says, grabbing Chris's arm and squeezing, "It is all because of her."

Anger and guilt rise in him and weaken his constitution.

His father lost his son, his wife, and now has lost himself.

Chapter Fourteen

His father's purple eyes hover in the air, unrecognizable and full of menace.

"If you ever wanted to punch your father," Chris says. "Now's the chance."

"I don't want to fight him," Scott answers before he understands why. His father's actions caused the night's terrors. He dug up the remains and brought them here. He gave Mr. Shirley the tomatoes that spread the disease. But he didn't know any of this would happen. Scott can not blame the man for his decisions anymore than Scott can blame himself for the decisions that lead to his mother's death. If he is going to forgive himself, he has to forgive his father. The man lost a son, a wife, and then watched his other son suffer. No matter how much Scott wanted revenge for every time his father punished him but didn't deserve it, he does not want to see his old man suffer any longer, especially since he is not in control of his actions.

The more Scott understands the nature of trauma, the more he realizes how little control anyone has over their lives.

The infected women's footfalls running down the hall draw closer. Chris nods to the other door and moves for it, but that door opens.

Sarah steps out.

Chris turns his face back toward Scott and then shifts his eyes toward Sarah. Scott understands and nods his head. They moved toward Sarah. Scott's father reaches for him, but he slips away. Sarah lunges at Chris, but he bends over, wraps his arms around her waist and lifts her into the air. He carries her into the room with Scott following and closing the door behind them.

The room is adorned with children's school desks and the walls are filled with posters of Bible quotes and crayon-colored artwork depicting scenes from it. A chalkboard sits on one end and a closet in another. This must be where kids go for religion studies.

On the far wall is a row of windows with a view to the cemetery. An iron fence surrounds the lush, grassy yard that houses the gravestones, slabs, and mausoleums. A tree grows in the middle of the yard. Its trunk is wide and its branches stretch out and make a thick canopy over the center of the cemetery. Although the darkness and rain make the outside barely visible, Scott realizes that the tree is moving, not swaying as if blown by the wind, but gyrating, the edges of it rippling. Think shadows reach from it and retract where the rain lands.

Scott moves closer to the window, past Chris, who has wrapped Sarah in a bear hug and struggles to keep her arms pinned to her sides.

"A little help here, Scotty."

Scott barely hears him as he walks up the glass. There is enough light spilling from the streets around the grounds to highlight the trunk. It helps him to see that the trunk is not dark because of a lack of light, but because it is mostly black, with hints of purple throughout.

"Scott!"

He turns around and moves in front of Sarah. He places his hands on her head and uses his new senses to connect with the disease. Seeing her with such angry eyes and torn skin creates a despair and anger that he had only felt since his mother's death. He will not let that happen again.

He tries to take the disease into himself as he had done before, but the entity inside is fighting, not wanting to let her go. He can sense that it knows how important she is to him, and wants to keep that relationship as an asset. The disease inside of himself squirms, sending pain through his body. With his concentration on her infection, he's losing the grip on his own.

Scott

Sarah's mind slips through as he plays tug-of-war with the entity.

"Sarah," he says aloud, wanting to be relieved but knowing he has yet to save her.

"Listen to my voice. Concentrate on pushing it out of you and into me. I'm immune to it. I can keep it from influencing my mind."

It's telling me terrible things.

"Ignore it, Sarah. It's trying to distract you. Make you weak."

It's too hard. It's showing me everything I fear. Losing my chances. Losing you. Losing both by trying to keep you both.

"It can only show you what might happen, not what will happen. You don't need to be afraid of something that hasn't happened yet."

But what if it does? What's the point of living if you might lose it all?

It's a question he has asked himself time and time again and still doesn't have an answer. Maybe there is no answer. Death is literally at the door, after all. He knows Sarah has been worried about her future, but never thought she would let it consume her. She excels at whatever life has had to offer. How could she not excel at anything else that comes her way?

He pulls her closer and kisses her forehead.

"Nothing is too hard for you. Don't let the fear of losing me come true before it happens."

The watch on his wrist catches his attention. She said that she custom made it for him with the ability to tell time as a metaphor, yet wouldn't tell him what that metaphor represent-ed. If he had taken the time to think about when he first saw it, he would say that time doesn't matter. That's a fantasy, of course, because time marches on whether you think about it or not.

"Time is irrelevant when I'm with you," she told him before she confessed her love for him.

Time marches on, but their love for each other remains.

"Our lives might not turn out exactly as we hope or plan, but what matters is that we are willing to try. If I can't go to college with you, then I will be there on the weekends to help you study. If you have to live miles away for a job, I'll visit you on your lunch break. I'll be with you every step of the way if you want me. I will be standing with you when you get married, and if the future sees you falling in love with another person, then I will stand by your side as your best man. The good things that can happen are just as valid as the bad. Concentrate on those possibilities, and know that whatever life throws at us, we are strong enough to survive it."

Scott feels Sarah's mind connect to his, a sensation he has not felt since the first time they kissed. He closes his eyes and feels her essence mix with his, and the world outside disappears. Their minds coalesce until there is no space for anyone elses to intrude. Scott and Sarah open their eyes. The ichor on her skin is gone and lying in a puddle on the classroom floor.

"That's what it's like for you all the time? The intrusive thoughts? The voice that is yours but isn't?"

"Yeah, but I think it's already getting better." He smiles, and she returns it with a kiss.

"I helped save you, too." Chris says.

Sarah smiles at him and feigns anger. "You told Scott I'm not your type."

"Oops," he shrugs.

An arm punches through the door.

"Plan?" Chris asks.

Scott looks at the tree in the yard. "That's where the body is. If I can destroy the disease in that I'm pretty sure it will stop everything it split itself into."

They look outside and then back toward the door. Scott's father's hand searches the doorknob for the lock.

"Go," Sarah says. "We'll by you time."

"I don't want to risk losing you again."

"You saved us. Now, let us save you."

Scott looks outside. If he can destroy the body, he might be able to save everyone.

"A good luck kiss before I go?" He asks.

Chris leans in and kisses him on his cheek.

"That's fair, I guess," Scott says.

He walks to the window and opens the middle panel.

"You are wrong about one thing," he says to Sarah before slipping through the window.

"What's that?" she asks.

"You already saved me."

CHAPTER FIFTEEN

PURPLE VISCERA SIZZLES AS it burns under the hard beam of his flashlight as he travels across the lawn. At the base of the unearthly tree is a tombstone.

Frances Holland
Beloved Wife & Devoted Mother

He lifts the light until he discovers an object imbedded into the bark at eye height. Its wood exterior and shape are obvious. A large portion of the disease lies inside the coffin, flowing outwards and creating the environment around the cemetery. He points the light inside and watches as some of the disease burns and some of it retracts out of fear, revealing pieces of white underneath. Sections of the skeleton; a crack ribcage, a tibia, a baby's skull. Its temple is cracked and missing a chunk of bone and its eyes sockets are empty and dark.

"Hello Brother," Scott says, sorrow replacing the fear in his heart. The connection he had been feeling as he drew closer to the source encompasses them now that they are finally in the same space.

Are you prepared to let me inside?

The voice in his head is not his own, though it still speaks with his voice. He hopes that he can silence this disgusting copy of his brother's mind.

"I'm prepared to help you move on."

Excruciating pain fills Scott's head and forces him to his knees. He feels the remnants of it growing inside of his body and getting stronger. He concentrates on subduing it as something wet wraps around his ankle. A slimy appendage jerks him into the air, loosening his grip on the flashlight and sending to the grass to be swallowed up by the disease. He hangs upside down in the air as black veins grow from the appendage and snake down his body. He fights against it with his mind while also kicking at it with his other foot.

Several tendrils of disease rise from the floor and twist into a solid object that ends in a sharp point and aims directly at his forehead. He tries to grab it, but it snakes away and pulls back. He kicks the tentacle around his ankle again, but it responds by squeezing tight enough to nearly shatter his bones.

Behind the tentacle, the skull's empty eye sockets fill with purplish light.

Why do you struggle?

"Because I'm not letting my fear control me anymore," he answers. The pain in Scott's leg is enough to start his adrenaline. Instead of fighting against the grip, he reaches up and digs his nails into the viscera. He yells as he claws through it, feeling as though he is ripping into his own skin. Blood and disease squirt onto his face and fly through the air. He rips apart the tentacle and his body drops. His head hits his mother's tombstone on the way down, cracking his skull and cutting into his forehead.

He cries out in pain as the tree shudders.

You're already half dead. Broken. Let me end your suffering.

"Oh, I'm just bleeding," he says with an ironic laugh. "I haven't even broken a sweat."

Scott rolls to his feet and uses his hands to lift himself onto the tombstone. The sharp tentacle spears forward, but he dives away in time. He rolls across the muck and the jumps forward to dig his hands into the coffin. He pulls chunks of it away, freeing his brother's tiny skeleton by the fistful. Pain shoots through his head with every pull, but he fights through it, screaming and clawing with ferocity until he is able to grab the skull from the coffin.

He looks into the sockets at the large purple infection that pulsates like a heart but acts like a brain.

I want to live, it tells Scott in his own voice. The voice makes him wonder if his brother would have grown up to sound exactly like him.

"You're not my brother. You infected his body and became part of him, but he's gone. I won't let you keep infecting his memory.

He lifts the skull to bring it down on top of the tombstone.

I was born into nothing, and existed in darkness. I want to live.

The words stop him. Even though this disease copied his brother's mind, his brother was a real person, regardless of how briefly he existed. He's scared, tortured by a life in darkness, and only wants to live.

You're right, Scott thinks to it, to his brother's mind. You were born, died, and what remained was left alone in the dark. I'm sorry that happened to you. I've been lucky enough to never have been left alone in the dark. I have a family that loves me, friends that stand beside me. I've never known true loneliness, absolute darkness. There has always been a speck of light, even in the darkest times. I'm going to give that light to you.

Scott digs his thumbs into the disease in each of the eye socket and concentrates on taking the disease into himself, away from his brother's remains completely. He closes his eyes and feels burning pain as the disease seeps into his pores. The tree and his body shake violently through tremendous pain. The disease across the yard pulls toward him. He opens his mouth to scream, but the treelike structure loses its solidity and drowns his body.

<hr>

SCOTT FLOATS IN ABSOLUTE darkness, unmoving, barely alive. Pain - physical and mental - is no longer a sensation. All that is left is nothingness.

He is surprised to feel that along with the nothingness comes a calmness. A certainty. A reprieve from the pangs of life......

<hr>

SCOTT OPENS HIS EYES. The pinks and yellows of dawn illuminate the cemetery.

The disease continues to coat the earth, black and sticky, but its purple hue is gone. He sees its lifelessness, but also feels the absence of its presence. The only part of the disease that has awareness is inside his body, but even that is melting away.

He looks around the yard and sees a bird land on top of the headstone. He feels its presence as though he is attuned to the bird, as though they share a bond. The heat of the rising sun tickles his skin and a cool breeze cools it back down and creates goose bumps, like its skin is feeling the air for the first time. The scent of flowers attack his sense of smell. The dew makes the greens of the cemetery glisten. The colors around him appear more vivid than he had ever seen.

He feels more present in the world than it has ever been. He feels...

Complete.

"Are you okay?" Sarah says from behind. He turns and sees her and Chris walking up the yard from the school window.

"Yes," he says, and is surprised to know he is telling the truth.

"You actually did it, didn't you?" Chris says.

Scott furrows his brow. "Actually?"

Sarah sits next to him. "What did you do?"

"I decided to give him what he wanted. I let him in."

"What?" Chris asks.

"I wanted to give him what I have." He looks between both of them.

"So where is he?" Sarah asks.

"I think he's part of me now."

Sarah lets that hang in the air and rests a head on his shoulder.

"Can we go home now?" Chris asks.

"Absolutely," Scott sighs, "but I have to do something first."

Scott crawls over to his mother's grave and kneels in front of her headstone.

"I never visited," he says, sadly. Sarah stands behind him and places a hand on his shoulder. Something wet licks his hand and he hopes Chris is not the one licking it. Bastion nuzzles his fingers and sits at his side. Chris stands next to them and lowers his head.

Scott lets the tears flow as he places a hand on the top of the tombstone. "Rest in peace, Mom. Your children are going to be okay." He takes his hand off and does not feel the need to place it on again.

EPILOGUE

RECONSTRUCTION

ALMOST EVERYONE CONNECTED TO the disease was healed, and in some ways, healthier than they had been before becoming infected. Scott buried Shadow's ashes in his brother's grave in the backyard and a regular funeral was held for Mr. Shirley. The line of parishioners was out the door and around the block. Every man and woman under his command had appeared to pay their respects. The stories they told were incredible. Heroic. Beautiful.

Everyone on Village Court helped rebuild the neighborhood. No one said a word to each other while they did it - no one needed to. The disease had connected them all at one point, and so they all understood what had transpired. Scott's father still does not talk about it.

Chris became an EMT and a firefighter for the town. Some patients he loses, some he saves. His heart and expertise are evolving and unwavering. He keeps a peridot necklace around his neck to remind him that even those he fails to save, he also helps.

Scott travels around the world, no longer hindered by compulsive or intrusive thoughts. Well, they still come from time to time, but he's in therapy and on some medications to help him battle the hereditary mental illness. He has yet to pick a college, but everyone assumes that being out in the world is all the fulfillment he needs.

As for me and Scott, we keep in contact as much as possible. We talk, write letters, and see each other when we are both not busy. Even if we ever fall out of romantic love, we will always love each other and keep each other close.

I have a doctorate in behavioral science and have started my own practice. Several of my colleagues balked at my desire to write what they consider to be a fiction novel, but someone needs to tell this story. Besides, we were all connected to each other's minds at one point, the book wrote itself.

As a woman of science and reason, I have to accept that there was a disease that was able to do the things it did. I might not have been supernatural, but it was more than natural, but... there is something else that tests my perspective of what happened.

Everyone infected by the disease no longer feels any connection to it or to each other, except for Scott and I. We know when we need to talk and feel each other's feelings without being in close proximity. I can pinpoint the area of the world he is in without knowing. Sometimes, I'll awaken from a nightmare and realize that it was Scott that was having it. I try to brush this off as an aftereffect of the disease since he and I got the brunt of it in the end, but what I find curious is that I feel someone waking him from his nightmares. A body of fur brushes his skin and then curls next to him as he falls back to sleep. Yes, he took Bastion in, but Bastion sleeps on the floor.

I just have to accept the possibility that the people who love you never stop protecting you.

I see Scott in my head sometimes, sitting in the dark in front of his open closet. He stares into the darkness as though it's staring back. He is no longer afraid. He smiles back at it and asks whatever is inside to "come out and play."

Afterword: The Monsters Have Names

The scariest parts of this novel are true.

I was first aware of the voice while standing in the hallway of my Middle School at age twelve. The bell to start class had rung, and I wasn't inside the room, but my locker happened to be next to it and the teacher was waiting for me, so I figured I was okay.

Or she doesn't care about you enough to get mad.

The voice manifested in front of me as though it was a physical entity, and in my mind's eye, it became trapped inside my backpack as I zippered it closed.

A bad thought... trapped inside... where it can grow worse if not set free.

I knew the thought was ridiculous, yet I was compelled to rectify the made-up consequences. I opened the bag, "saw" the thought slither out, and closed the bag when it hovered far enough away from the zipper.

Sometimes the thoughts did not leave so easily.

I unzipped bags, opened and closed doors, and switched lights on and off until I was confident that the last thought I had when I left an object was positive and affirming. When I was in a good mood, I would only have to repeat the action a few times, but if I was sad, I could be performing those rituals for several minutes. Sometimes, over an hour. At the time, I did not know that I suffered from a chemical imbalance that caused anxiety and depression, so being in a sad mood was often the case.

My mental hurdles made me tired, depressed, and weak in body and spirit.

All the time.

Every day.

There was no internet to look up to see if others experienced these thoughts or feelings, and no one around me could understand how much I was hurting no matter how many times I tried to explain what I felt.

"You need more sleep."

"You need better nutrition."

"It's just puberty."

Not until I was in my twenties did I discover that I had a mental illness called Obsessive Compulsive Disorder. Not only were my symptoms identifiable, they were treatable. Maybe even curable.

Which brings me to my next fact about the story you just read: The happiest parts of this story are true.

I survived the ordeal because of an incredible amount of love and optimism. No matter how difficult life had become I moved through it with the strength, strong will, and hope instilled by my Mom and Dad, and from my brother, who is someone I still look up to when I need a reminder that there is at least one hero in the world.

That's what this novel is about. Survival, and the people who see you through your weakest moments.

Scott is based on me, and Sarah and Chris are based on two specific people, Suzanne Adams and Chris Belmont. Although the romance between Scott and Sarah is fabricated for story purposes, their love is not. Suzanne's friendship helped me find the strength to endure my troubles. When the symptoms of my OCD, anxiety, and depression were at their worst, I reminded myself that if an intelligent, beautiful, funny girl called me her best friend, then surely I must be worthy of life. I will be forever grateful for that gift.

Chris is the type of friend every kid should have growing up, a strong-willed chaotic teddy who is as full of humor as he is heart. I remember us fighting monsters on my front lawn when we were kids. He helped me fight off real monsters over the years. No matter how far apart we live or how long we go without seeing each other, he will never be far from my mind and heart. He will forever be my brother.

How many nights did the three of us spend together, feeling the weight of the world on our shoulders? I hope this book has expressed how much of that weight you carried for me.

When I was out of college, I met Kathleen, a scientist as loving and kind as she is intelligent. I was smitten with her and terrified that my wounded mind would ruin our budding relationship. I confessed to her my ailments, but instead of being horrified, she not only recognized each one, she told me their names.

"Anxiety."

"Depression."

"Obsessive Compulsive Disorder."

Kathleen helped me find specialists to help me heal. We have been together for sixteen years and have a beautiful daughter named Evelyn, and a handsome beast of a cat named Dusty. To say that my life was never the same after I met her is an understatement. Kathleen healed my wounds and saved my life.

I've been through some horrible, terrifying things because of the chemical imbalances in my brain. Yet, here I am, at forty years old, happier and healthier than ever.

When I first sat down to write this, my family was sitting together in the living room when my seven-year-old daughter looked at her mother and said, "Sometimes, when I turn around one way, I have to turn back around, or else it doesn't 'feel right.'" My wife looked at me, both of us slack-jawed and pale-faced. Were her words just part of childhood imagination, or a sign that we passed down something terrifying to our child?

"It doesn't matter," my wife reminded me. "We will be there for her."

We have fought those monsters, continue to fight those monsters, and they will not win. Our daughter will never have to face those monsters alone.

If you or anyone you know is experiencing any of these ailments, please reach out for help. The one aspect of this novel I want people to take away is that there is always hope.

Always.

I could keep writing about my experience because this ailment has haunted me my entire life, but the only voice I hear that matters comes from my daughter as she runs around the front yard, calling for me to come out and play.

Patrick Tumblety, 2024

SPECIAL THANKS AND ACKNOWLEDGMENTS

This book is in your hands because of Candace Nola. I could never thank her enough for believing in this story and me. The support every writer dreams about is the support she and Uncomfortably Dark Horror have shown me during my first novel publication. Thank you for making my dream come true.

To Erin Sweet Al-Mehairi, for her work on what became the final version of the book, as well as Christine Hughes and Dan Hanks for their work on different versions of this story.

To my wife and daughter, for their love, and for recognizing when I have "that look" while staring at my computer and giving me time and space to write. Your patience and understanding are immeasurable.

To Grant, for championing my writing and giving me confidence throughout the years. Thank you for coming with me on this journey and helping me find my voice. (Also, thanks to Katy and Piper for supporting us!)

To Burt, Adam, and Jon for your constant love and support.

To my mom, dad, and brother, for supporting me as an artist and giving me the strength to follow my dreams.

Patrick Tumblety is featured in numerous horror, science-fiction, and poetry anthologies. Besides writing, he creates multimedia art, teaches self-defense, and plays video, card, and board games. He has an unhealthy obsession with Batman. Patrick resides with his wife, daughter, and cat in Delaware.